ANNA SPARROWS

Matteo's Mettle

Littles & Lace Book 2

Cover Design by: Ky at Blue Brolli Graphics

First edition

This book was professionally typeset on Reedsy.
Find out more at reedsy.com

To the wonderful people who picked up Asher's Answer and demanded Book 2, you all rock!
I wish you all the Daddies (and/or Littles) of your dreams. Or of mine. Either works, really.
insert wink emoji here

Contents

Preface	ii
Chapter One – Matteo	1
Chapter Two – London	11
Chapter Three – Matteo	20
Chapter Four – London	33
Chapter Five – Matteo	46
Chapter Six – London	56
Chapter Seven – Matteo	68
Chapter Eight – London	80
Chapter Nine – Matteo	91
Chapter Ten – London	102
Chapter Eleven – Matteo	118
Chapter Twelve – London	126
Chapter Thirteen – Matteo	139
Chapter Fourteen – London	149
Chapter Fifteen – Matteo	159
Epilogue – London	165
Sneak Peek: Ted's Temerity	177
About the Author	186
Also by Anna Sparrows	188

Preface

This is Book 2 of the *Littles & Lace* series, however it can be read as a standalone.

Please bear in mind that, while this is a low-angst, sweet & cute, instant-attraction romance, this book does contain brief mentions of cruelty and bigotry, as well as anxiety and panic attacks.

Similarly, this book is an MM Age Play/Age Regression romance between consenting adults with a **significant age gap** (younger Daddy, older Little) and **does** include ABDL and wetting, as well as descriptions of men wearing lingerie.

I am still a firm believer in not yucking someone else's yum, so if these kinks aren't for you, don't read them.

Life's too short to read something you don't enjoy.

Chapter One — Matteo

J ust under two years ago, I reached the lowest point of my life. I'd turned forty-three and my Daddy, a man I'd been with for almost a decade, sat me down and told me that our relationship wasn't working for him anymore. Heartbroken didn't quite cover how I felt.

I'd given that man the prime years of my life and he was ending it without any warning. Hell, the night before had been just like any other. We'd had sex, exchanging words of affection as always, and then we'd gone through my little night-time routine. Bath time, diapering, a bedtime story, and a bottle as I snuggled up alongside him. It was the same routine he had set when we first got together, when I was new to the world of BDSM and kink play.

I was a late bloomer, I guess. Imagine being in your thirties and discovering sides of yourself you'd never known were there.

Ladies and gentlemen, I give you Matteo Brightman: dense as fuck.

So, yeah. Daddy had sat me down three weeks after my forty-third birthday and ended our relationship. Just like that. He'd been clinical and impassive about it, hinting that I wasn't the kind of Little he wanted anymore. Not as I inched towards my mid-forties. Not with my bulky build and tattooed skin – changes I'd made over the course of the decade which he had been wholly supportive of at the time. I understood. I was graying at the temples, and I was physically too big and 'masculine' to fit the 'Little' stereotype. Still, surely ten years of togetherness should have meant *something* to him?

Spoiler alert: it did not.

Unfortunately, nothing I said moved him. He hadn't reacted to my tears, either. That had cemented the whole breakup for me. If Daddy was impassive in the face of my tears, things really were over.

The only friends I had were all his to start with; people in the lifestyle he had introduced me to. None had been willing to 'get in the middle' of our breakup by allowing me to couch surf. I spent one night at a colleague's place, then called my dad and arranged to move back in with him until I could sort my shit out. The only issue with that was moving halfway across the country.

I'd seen it as a win, though. A fresh start away from the reminder of my shattered heart and ruined life. As an electrical engineer, finding another job near Dad's place wasn't too difficult. Starting my whole life over again at forty-three? That turned out to be much harder.

Especially when Dad died from a sudden heart attack three months after I moved in.

The only thing that consoled me in my grief was that I'd had those three months with him. If Trent —my Daddy— hadn't dumped me when he did, I would never have moved back home. In some ways, I was glad that the end of my relationship had given me those last few months with my father.

Following Dad's death, I threw myself into work. I'd inherited his house (the one I'd grown up in) and, when I wasn't working, I was doing small renovations. It was both rewarding and necessary. I had needed to make the space my own as part of my grieving process. Close to three months following his death, I discovered The Grove.

It had happened by complete accident. One of the guys at work had mentioned it under his breath. The Grove had hired our company to update their high-tech monitoring systems and the teams working on the project had all had to sign hefty non-disclosure agreements. Craig, a younger, kind of arrogant engineer, had been in the employee break room with another member of their team, muttering derisively about 'fetishists' and 'kinky freaks' under his breath while I'd been waiting for my lunch to heat up in the microwave.

My ears had perked up immediately, my stomach swooping with hope.

It had been six months since I had truly indulged my kinky urges. Before Dad had died, I'd tried a couple of BDSM clubs in the city, but my experiences had not been positive. It turned out Trent wasn't the only Daddy who thought I was too big and too old to be a Little. I'd been beginning to wonder if maybe they were right.

Unfortunately, though, my heart (and dick) weren't giving up on my interests or my needs. This was who I was always going to be. A Little. I had an inherent need to be cherished and cared for and, yeah, *babied*...for lack of a better word.

I loved having a Daddy to play with me, bathe me, diaper

and dress me. I loved having my decisions —when I wasn't at work— taken care of for me. My food chosen and cut up for me, my entertainment arranged by someone else. It made the maelstrom of stressful thoughts in my head cease.

And the fact that I enjoyed the sexual aspect of the Daddy/Little boy dynamic? That was the cherry on top.

Well, it had been in my thirties. Before I'd bulked up. Trent had been a gym rat and, with nothing else to do but follow along, I'd discovered that I enjoyed weight training, too. He had supported it. Had even said that he loved how big and strong I was becoming. He'd always had a thing for buff men. He hadn't ever complained that it made it more difficult to find onesies and Little clothes that fit properly, or that I was beginning to look ridiculous wearing them.

Not until he dumped my sorry ass, anyway.

So heading back out into the community into a new city where I didn't know anybody else involved the lifestyle was rough. Most Daddies aren't into a boy who could bench press them, or who 'looks like a sad reject from *Sons of Anarchy*' if the guy I'd met at my first club's assessment was to be believed. I felt lost and alone, and indulging in cartoons at home in a diaper I'd put on myself was a cold comfort at best.

Would The Grove be able to offer anything that the other clubs had not? It had sounded like it was a more professional establishment, if the NDAs our company had needed to sign were any indication, but I was wary.

Still, I reached out to them anyway. Meg, one of the three women who manned the front desk, had been so sweet and helpful. She'd answered all my questions and invited me to the next dedicated Littles' Night where they would open the doors to non-members (after a vetting process) to check out the space and interact with other caregivers and Littles. The club would also organize a variety of fun activities for the evening as part of the themed event. I signed up on the spot.

Even though I didn't meet any potential Daddies that night, I made a connection with another buff Little. Josh Walker. When I'm little, I'm painfully shy, but that hadn't stopped the guy from plopping down beside me at the pottery station and chatting my ears off. By the end of the night, I'd left with a smile on my face and a new friend's contact number in my phone.

However, while Josh introduced me to his brother and his friends in kink community, I still longed to find a Daddy of my own.

Hell, eighteen months on from that and I'm still lonely as fuck.

Maybe it's just time to hang up my onesies and settle for a vanilla relationship. As much as I hate that idea, I hate the idea of being alone forever even more.

"Earth to Matt," my friend and fellow Little, Ash, waves his hand in my face. I'm at the house he shares with his Daddy and fiancé, Charlie, and we've been playing with blocks in the living room.

These playdates have been happening ever since Josh introduced me to the guys. Charlie also happens to be Josh's older brother, and they have a close-knit social circle of kinky friends. Even now, I'm still amazed that they invited me to be a part of it.

Charlie, a former cop, has also been kind enough to be my caregiver during these playdates. He's a decade my junior, but he's got Daddy vibes for days. To be honest, I've always been mildly envious of Asher (who is in his early twenties, has a slender, athletic frame and guileless wide hazel eyes) for his luck finding such a perfect Daddy. Not that I'd be Charlie's type, obviously, but I badly want what they share together.

I don't allow myself to regress too far with Charlie. I don't need him changing me or giving me a bottle. But he does cut up my meals while I'm here and cuddle me on the couch when the three of us enjoy story-time. It's the most bitter-sweet feeling: I get a taste of the life I want, but I also know this isn't really mine to enjoy.

"Matt?"

I give myself a shake at Ash's repetition of my name. Biting my lip, I offer him a sheepish grin. "Sorry. I was just thinking."

Ash frowns and cocks his head. "About?"

He's not overly little today, either. He tends to be more fluid in the way he drifts in between his Little and Big personas, but it is unusual that he's not letting go during our playdate. I feel a bit guilty, because I can see his concern for me written all over his expressive face and I'm guessing that's what's keeping him from losing himself.

Great. Now I'm bringing him down, too.

With a sigh, I drop the orange cylindrical block I've been fiddling with for the last few minutes and shrug. "Nothing important."

His eyes narrow. After observing me for a moment longer, he looks up and over my shoulder, where Charlie's lounging on the couch with a book. "Charlie, we're done here," he declares without any trace of his Little self in his words and unfolds himself from his cross-legged position with a grace I wish I could emulate. He climbs to his feet and dusts imaginary lint off his play shorts. Then he offers me his hand.

Taking it, I groan as he helps pull me to my feet where I tower over him. My knees and back protest painfully. Another sign that maybe I really am getting too old for this. I can't quite school my face in time, and I know that Ash catches the flicker of mourning I just felt.

Still eyeing me carefully, he says, "Let's get changed, then grab a beer."

It's more a demand than a suggestion.

Nodding, I head towards the guest bathroom upstairs where I left my adult clothes and can hear Charlie and Ash murmuring quietly as I go. When I meet them back in the kitchen a handful of minutes later, their combined worry for me is almost palpable.

I offer Charlie a grateful "Thank you" when he hands me a bottle of pale ale, the cap already popped.

Ash and Charlie let me take a deep draw from the amber bottle before Charlie asks, "What's going on?"

I look back across the kitchen island at him. He's got his arm wrapped around Ash, but his eyes are narrowed on me. He and I are close in height and build, where Ash is a handful of inches shorter. Charlie's got a neatly trimmed, thick dark beard and startlingly blue eyes. He's a handsome man, and Ash is equally pretty. Nestled together as they are, they make a beautiful couple and my heart aches with jealousy and loneliness even more.

Get it together, Brightman.

"It's nothing," I try to brush off the question, but these guys know me better than that by now.

While we might only have been in each other's lives for eighteen months or so, I like to think that we've gotten close. I would say that I have connected more with them and Josh than with the other guys in our social circle. It comes from spending so much time on playdates with Ash, I suppose.

As expected, Charlie scoffs. "*Matteo...*" He goes full Daddy, all stern and expectant.

He's not my Daddy, but with all the time we've spent together with him as my proxy caregiver, I'm still wired to respond.

"Ugh, that's a sneaky tactic, asshole," I tilt the neck of my beer bottle at him in accusation and he raises an eyebrow, not wavering. *Damn it.* Swallowing roughly, I look up at the ceiling. "I'm just all up in my head right now. I'm feeling..." *Lost. Alone. Hopeless. Broken. Pathetic.* "...tired."

Charlie's expression remains neutral as he continues to observe me in silence. I pick at the label on my beer bottle, averting my eyes under his scrutiny. But it's not him who speaks next. It's Ash.

"You're lonely."

Even though they're delivered softly and with obvious compassion, the words seem to echo around us and I flinch. My shoulders lift and droop in a shrug, and now I really can't meet either of their gazes.

Running my finger through the condensation dripping down the bottle in my hand, I try to brush the whole thing off. "It's just...I don't know...like a midlife crisis. It's stupid."

I'll be turning forty-five in another week, and I assume that's been a trigger for these feelings. Another birthday to spend on my own. Another sign that I'm aging out of the lifestyle I enjoy so deeply.

Forty-five. Fucking hell.

"It's not stupid," Ash argues, slipping out of Charlie's embrace and circling the kitchen island. He wraps one of his arms around me and pulls my head down to his shoulder. I hate myself for soaking up the affection like a sponge. "Have you thought about—"

"I'm not going back again." This I am firm on. "Every time I go, it's the same shit. I can't…"

Fuck it.

My voice breaks, and my throat clogs with tears. The truth is, I can't handle constantly being told what I know deep in my bones: I'm not a desirable Little. And it stings all the more that I'm about to have this breakdown on the shoulder of a *perfect* Little. I shouldn't resent him for his youth or his slimmer frame, but some part of me does, and that makes me feel like an incredibly shitty friend on top of everything else.

It's bad enough that I'm jealous of the relationship he and Charlie have, but being envious of his appearance? What am I, twelve? I give myself a mental shake and go back to the issue at hand.

The clientele at The Grove are certainly of a higher caliber than at the other clubs in the city, but the rejection there has been hurtful all the same. Even at The Grove, or in the online groups Josh and Ash suggested I join, the Daddies are looking for cute, sweet Littles. *Littles like Ash.* They're usually kind about turning down my advances, but I don't have it in me to try anymore.

"I'm done." I say into the silence that has once again descended. My voice is shaky, and I can feel my heart breaking, already grieving the life I've decided to say goodbye to. "I'm giving up age play."

Ash gasps, and out of the corner of my eye I watch his hand fly to his mouth.

Across the kitchen island, Charlie's voice is low and equally surprised. "Matt…"

Forcing myself to look up, I steel my jaw. Looking between

them, I shake my head. "I've been thinking about this for a while. I need to walk away from it."

I'm surprised by how convinced I sound to my own ears.

If only my heart would get with the program.

Chapter Two — London

"Y**ou are a life saver,"** my best friend, Cherie, tells me as she lets me in through the front door of her apartment. She looks harried, with dark circles under her brown eyes, and wisps of her honey blonde hair escaping from the messy bun on top of her head.

I pin her with a firm stare. "You need to find a new job."

She's currently working as a PA for a local politician and, as far as I am concerned, the guy is an epic douchebag. He calls her at all hours with outrageous demands, and because she can't afford not to work right now she jumps at his every beck and call. He's taking advantage, and I hate him.

Abject misery washes over her face. "I know. I've started applying."

"Thank fuck for that."

"London, language," she scolds, launching into what I call her 'Mommy mode'.

I chuckle and shake my head. "That might work on your cute little wife, Cher, but not on me."

Which brings us back to why I'm here at all. Cherie promised her wife, Kate, that she would take her to this month's Littles' Night at The Grove (which is happening tonight) and, naturally, her dickwad boss has jumped up and down with a last-minute emergency that Cherie needs to fix immediately. When she called me an hour ago, she sounded close to tears.

Never one to cope well with anyone being upset, let alone my best friend, I told her I'd happily take Kate. Being 'cool Uncle London' has always been fun, and it's about time I checked out the club that my girls are so fond of.

Cherie pins me with an intense stare. "Are you sure you're okay with this? It's one thing to be around Kate when she's little, but something completely different to go to a kink club for a themed night."

"Hey, you know me," I shrug. "I'm easy. Am I particularly kinky? No." Well, not that she's aware. My penchant for lace underwear is a secret nobody knows about. Not even my exes, and certainly not my best friend. It's something I indulge in in private. "But do I yuck other peoples' yum? Also no." My lips curl upwards into my standard winning grin. "Besides, Kate said it's Disney night tonight. I'm not missing that. My girl and I are going to get our Disney on together."

Cherie still doesn't look convinced. "I'm serious," she insists. "It can be a bit full-on. And I know you're good with our lifestyle, but you're still so young and—"

"Whoa," I hold up my index finger to silence her, then point it at her. "Since when has my age ever bothered you?" She's in her mid-thirties, while I'm twenty-six.

We met at college, where she was auditing one of my classes, and exchanged sarcastic barbs about the professor of the class while seated next to each other in the back row of the lecture hall. From there a friendship was born, with the two of us bonding over both being a part of the LGBTQ+ community in addition to loathing lazy college professors who read directly from the textbook.

I was the first person she introduced Kate to, the first person with whom they publicly explored their Mommy/girl relationship, and her Best Man at their wedding last year. As far as I'm aware, my age has never made a difference to her.

Hell, Kate's only two years older than me anyway.

As if Cherie can read all of these thoughts on my face, her own falls and she appears stricken at the words that left her own lips. She scrubs her perfectly manicured hand over her face. "I know, I know; I'm sorry. I don't even know why I said that."

I can't even stay mad at her. Pulling her into a hug, I justify it for her. "You're tired. Overworked. Overwhelmed. Stressed as fuck. And you feel guilty because you can't take your girl to the one thing she's been looking forward to for weeks."

Cherie allows herself one broken sob against me before she pulls back and puts herself back together. That shit's not healthy, either, but I'm not telling her that. She has to work tonight, after all.

Even if I was going to say something, the chance is broken by the loud squeal of my name from just down the hallway. "Uncle London!"

I turn, grinning at the sight of Kate in her costume for the evening. And that's what it is: an actual Disney costume. She's gone full princess, wearing a big, poofy yellow ballgown and has her dark brown hair piled atop her head with loose tendrils framing her rounded face.

Seeing as she's already in Little mode, I'm down to play along.

13

"Excuse me, Belle, but I'm actually looking for my Little niece, Katie. Have you seen her?"

Her giggles warm me from the inside and I share a fond look with Cherie, whose eyes glisten with telling tears. She really needs to leave that job.

"Uncle London, it *is* me," Kate insists in that exaggerated 'you're an idiot' tone that most three-year-olds have down pat. She spins around, the sweeping skirts of her dress fanning out with the movement. "Mommy had this made 'specially for me so I can be Belle."

When they first started exploring their kink, Cherie confessed that Kate was particularly self-conscious about being a plus-sized Little. Finding Little clothes was, in and of itself, a fairly niche market. Finding Little clothes for plus-sized women —especially girls like Kate who loved all things Disney and princessy— was even more difficult. I've told Cherie on more than one occasion that she and I should go into business together to fill the hole in the market.

Shooting Cherie a quick glance that once again conveys this idea, I look back at Kate and smile indulgently. "It's perfect. You look *just* like Belle. But," I gasp dramatically, putting my hand on my chest, "if you're Beauty, does that make me the *Beast*?"

This earns me the desired reaction of loud peals of laughter, clapped hands and enthusiastic agreement. She throws her arms around me and stares up at me with her big, brown eyes. "Please, Uncle London? Can we be Beauty and the Beast? Even if you do look more like Gaston."

I'm never able to deny her. "I'll be your Beast, little one. But only because I love you." Then I cock my head to the side, as if I'm only just registering her last words, then I waggle my index finger at her. "But if you liken me to Gaston again, I don't know how long that love will last."

More giggles erupt from my Little friend.

Cherie's expression is convoluted – a mixture of fond adoration and blatant guilt. Unwilling to make this harder on her, I gesture for Kate to head towards the door. "Alright, Mommy, I have a princess to take to the ball, and I don't want our carriage to turn into a pumpkin."

Kate snorts and tells me that's the wrong movie, but it gets us moving out into the hallway. I wave off Cherie's effusive thanks and tell her I'll have her girl back home in a few hours. Then Kate grabs my hand and drags me to my car, chattering about how much fun we're going to have for the entire drive to the club.

When we get to The Grove, Kate gets impatient at the reception desk. She's already a member, but I am not. As it is Littles' Night, I don't have to be, but I do have to sign the requisite non-disclosure agreements, listen to the club's rules, acknowledge the house safe word ('turmeric') and sign a temporary membership and indemnity form. I'm impressed by all of this, knowing how exclusive this club is, and it makes me glad that they take the safety of their members so seriously.

"*Katie.*" My tone is firmer than I've ever had to use it when my best friend's wife tries pulling me away from the desk.

The woman at the reception desk has just finished explaining the 'flagging' system and is trying to wrap my chosen wrist-bands around my wrist. Kate put hers on when she signed in. I'm flagging as a Daddy, seeing as I'm Katie's caregiver for the evening, 'taken'/not interested in open play, and interested in men. It's a bit strange to literally wear it all on my sleeve like this, but I can understand the reasoning for the practice. No misunderstandings. Everyone stays comfortable and safe. It works.

When I turn back to face Kate, she's staring at me in awe.

"What?" I ask her.

"That was the best Daddy voice *ever*," she declares.

I shrug her observation off. "I learned it from your Mommy, I guess."

She shoots me a speculative look, but doesn't say anything more on the topic, distracted by the concierge telling us we're good to go through to the club.

It's an entire massive warehouse building on the edge of the city, right on the cusp of the industrial area. As soon as the large, metal door inside the reception space is opened, a wave of bass and music assaults us. Stepping through those doors, there's a central club space with a dance floor, dimly lit booths lining the walls, and a large stage at the end of the room. But, branching off to our left and right are two matching corridors which Kate says house the change rooms, lockers and bathrooms, and these wrap around the main club space to meet at the back of the building where we find a large staircase and two elevators to take us to the second floor.

We head up in one of the elevators and are greeted by a space that feels more reminiscent of a fancy hotel, with two parallel hallways directly in front of us. The rooms along here, Kate tells me as she tugs me along, are the playrooms. All themed and available for private play. At the end of the hallway, she pushes open a door and we step through into the Littles' playroom.

My jaw drops. This space has to take up at least a quarter of the entire second floor of the warehouse, running the entire width of the building. At the far end from the door we've just entered through, there's an honest-to-God bouncy castle which fills up the space from floor to ceiling. It's clearly sturdy enough to hold at least three adults, if the people currently bouncing on it are any indication.

The rest of the room is brightly lit by warm yellow lighting suspended high above our heads. The walls are painted bright colors, there are toys and activity stations all over the space, and there's a line of couches down the left side of the room where caregivers are lounging and chatting, elevated from the expansive playroom floor, giving them a good view of their Littles.

Tonight, Disney songs are playing through speakers mounted on the walls, but not so loud that the 'kids' (for lack of a better word) can't chatter and play together comfortably. And, because it's a themed Littles' night, there are specific activities being manned by club staff, like the 'Princess Makeup' group Kate drags me into. She plops down on her presumably padded backside (I can't tell if she's wearing a diaper under the voluminous mass of her ballgown, but she usually does when she's little) next to a Little dressed like Elsa, complete with wig. They appear masculine, but I'm not going to interrupt in order to clarify.

"Katie!" they squeal and hug her. "You're Belle!"

"Uh huh," she replies, beaming and smoothing her hands down the mass of tulle and satin, "Mommy got it 'specially for me."

"Your Mommy's the best," they sigh dreamily. They're probably about my age. Blonde bangs poke out from under the white wig, accompanied by bright green eyes, a cute button nose, and a five o'clock shadow across a soft, oval jawline. "My Daddy bought me the hair, but I made my dress myself."

"Benny, you need to start selling them," Kate insists, and it sounds like this is something she's told them before.

The woman running the makeup station (tall, reed thin, wearing kitten ears, a skin-tight black pleather leotard and a tail instead of a Disney costume) interrupts to give Kate a smock and a makeup palette. Seeing as she's settling in without any drama, I tell her I'm going to go sit with some of the other caregivers, and she waves me away without a backwards glance.

I take the opportunity to explore the space further first. It's kitted out like a giant day care center, and all the Littles clearly love it. It's no wonder that the membership fees for this place are so high. The club itself, from what I've seen, has spared no expense in the experiences it provides its members. It's enough to make me curious about seeing some of the other themed rooms someday.

"...can't believe you've talked me into this," a pleasantly mellow voice, sounding incredibly petulant, catches my ear.

Another male voice, pitched a little higher, laughs. "Just enjoy your birthday like a good boy, Matty. I promise, if this last-ditch effort fails, Charlie, Ash and I will drop it and you can hang up your diapers for good, okay?"

"*Ugh*," the first voice grumbles, but I can't hear much heat in it. "Fine."

"I still think you're crazy for wanting to do that, you know."

This time, the first voice —Matty— growls and I can hear the frustration in his words, "Drop it, Josh."

I turn around from the elaborate train set I've been pretending to inspect, intrigued by the conversation I've accidentally eavesdropped on. My curiosity has been piqued. Scanning the area near the 'paint a plaster character' table, my eyes land on the two men I assume were the ones I just overheard.

Holy fuck, they're hot.

Neither one of them looks like any of the other Littles in the room. They're both *built*, with giant-ass biceps and broad shoulders. The younger of the pair is wearing a tight Buzz Lightyear costume. His jaw is squared, covered in carefully trimmed stubble, and his eyes are dark brown. His hair is a standard 'short back and sides, slightly more on top' cut.

The older guy is wearing a onesie with Eeyore on the front. His face is rounder than the young guy's and he has a neat, dark beard that is liberally speckled with gray and silver which offset wide green eyes spectacularly. His hair is longer, too. A little shaggy around his ears and down towards his neck. It's also graying at the temples. His skin is a deliciously golden tanned color that makes my mouth water. And those huge arms of his? They're covered in a collection of dark ink, some faded and some clearly more recent. I want to get closer to check out the designs.

The older guy senses my stare and looks up to catch me appraising him. Considering how big and rugged he appears, I'm surprised by the blush that creeps over his cheeks and up the back of his neck. It's ridiculously adorable. He offers me the most beautiful, shy smile before he glances at his companion, then back to me. The smile falters then slides off his face.

My heart tugs painfully when he drops his eyes back down to his hands, which are fiddling with a plaster character I can't quite discern the shape of.

Frowning, I step forward, but I'm quickly distracted by Kate calling out for me. I sigh as I make my way back toward the makeup activity, hoping that I'll be able to seek out the guy in the Eeyore onesie again soon.

I just want to see that smile return to his face.

Chapter Three — Matteo

I feel like a dirty old man.

No, really, I am *a dirty old man.*

The kid I was just eyeing off can't be more than twenty-five. That's twenty years my junior. But, *hot damn*, he was attractive. From my spot on the floor, he appeared tall and solid. Not exactly gym-toned muscular, but stocky, with piercing blue eyes and thick black hair in a kind of coiffed style. His friendly face was squared and clean shaven, and home to his plump, kissable lips. And for a moment, the briefest moment, I thought he'd been checking me out.

But that's absurd. I'm sitting next to Josh, who convinced me that Littles' Night being scheduled for my birthday was *a sign*, and it's more likely that the hot young Daddy was checking him out considering he's much more age appropriate for the guy.

"Seen anyone you wanna play with?" Josh asks, his tongue poking out of the side of his mouth as he concentrates on painting the Mickey Mouse plaster figure he selected.

Yes. A hot as fuck Daddy who I'm probably old enough to have actually fathered. Y'know, if I'd ever swung that way.

I sigh. "No. It looks like the usual crowd."

Josh looks up and scans the room. It's gotten busy, which isn't a surprise considering the theme of the evening. He frowns before he turns to arch an eyebrow at me. "I see a few new faces."

"Can't you just leave it?" I haven't even started painting the Donald Duck figurine I chose. "It's my birthday, and I'm really not in the mood to be rejected tonight."

He rolls his eyes and points his paintbrush at me, a glob of red paint wobbling dangerously on the end. "Those are big words for someone who's s'posed to be little."

Tears sting the back of my eyes as a lump lodges in my throat. I'm at war within myself. I haven't been able to sink into my Little headspace properly in months. I want to; I really, truly do. But months of hearing 'you're too old', 'you're too big', 'you look like a Dom' have taken their toll. I'm on edge here in the club, feeling the stares and judgment from those around me, but being little at home without a Daddy has lost its appeal, too.

"Fuck, Matt, I'm sorry," Josh tosses his paintbrush down, splattering the paper-covered table with red paint, and pulls me into a hug. "You can be as little or big as you want."

It takes me a moment to get my shit together, and when I pull away from his hug, I force a smile. "I'm just having a midlife crisis," I jest, repeating the same words I've been using to describe my dilemma for a while now, "don't mind me."

"It's your birthday; you can cry if you want to."

"I don't think that's the right lyric."

"I'm paraphrasing."

Josh's blasé attitude about misquoting a classic tune has my lips twitching with amusement. "Just let me paint my duck in peace, would you?"

"You're the boss." He settles back in to his masterpiece without further argument, for which I'm beyond thankful.

I forget all about the hot Daddy for the better part of the next hour, managing to finally slip into Littlespace. Josh drags me from one activity to another, and eventually I have to admit that I'm having fun.

Can I really give this up?

I know the guys won't shun me if I take a step back from the lifestyle, but will I really be happy hanging out with them if I do? Will I be able to watch Ash being little for Charlie, or listen to Josh's outlandish stories of how bratty he can be without it feeling like torture? Not to mention how much harder it might become if Chance, Spence and Ted also find their forever Littles. Can I really sit among that and not miss being a part of it?

No. I don't think I can.

Which means that walking away from being little includes walking away from the friends I've made here.

I don't want to do that. But, at the same time, I don't want to be living in limbo, either.

A loud, infectious laugh pulls me out of my spiraling thoughts. I instinctively turn towards the sound. My breath catches in my throat when I realize that the laughter is coming from the hot young Daddy I locked eyes with earlier.

"Who's that?" I can't help asking Josh, pointing in the Daddy's direction.

Josh puts down the Play-Doh he'd been shaping into a giant penis and *not* the Disney characters we're supposed to be

22

building and follows the line from my index finger. Hot Young Daddy (as I am now calling him, because I'm clearly very creative) is standing with a group of caregivers, watching as a bunch of Littles engage in a 'dance off' set to Disney songs.

Thankfully, Josh and I both agreed that that particular activity was not for us.

"*Hellooo Daddy*," my friend says, all low and husky as he drags the words out, his eyes lighting up as they land on the man in question. He lets out an appreciative whistle. "I've never seen him here before…and, believe me, I'd remember if I had."

I snort.

Casting me a sideways glance, Josh's expression turns sly. "I didn't know you liked 'em young, Matty. He's gotta be about my age."

I refuse to blush. I refuse to blush. I refuse to…damn it.

My cheeks flame.

"Shut up. I don't usually."

And I don't. I mean, I appreciate attractive men of all ages, but I've never been into younger Daddies. Of course, at my age, most of the guys in the club are at least a decade my junior now, and I can't be upset at being rejected for my age while simultaneously rejecting potential Daddies for theirs. That's just hypocritical. Still, this guy is *young* young. Like he's probably still getting asked for his ID at bars young.

Josh turns to look Hot Young Daddy over again. "Pity his bands say he's not looking to play."

My gaze drifts to Hot Young Daddy's wrist and my heart sinks. I should have figured someone as attractive as him would be taken.

"But he's gay, so all is not lost." Josh observes. His tone takes on a hopeful lilt. "Maybe he's not actually with anyone? Maybe he just wanted to check out the club without pressure?"

I shake my head, arching an eyebrow. "You're an eternal optimist, aren't you?"

Josh shrugs but doesn't turn back to look at me. He's still staring unashamedly at Hot Young Daddy. Then his brows furrow. "If he's gay, why's he here with a girl?"

"What?" I swivel my head back around so quickly I'm surprised I don't give myself whiplash. Sure enough, Hot Young Daddy is now cuddling a curvaceous Little in a stunning Belle ballgown costume. Whatever was left of my hopes crashes and burns. I sigh. "Maybe Meg handed him the wrong band."

"Hmm," Josh doesn't sound convinced. "Meg's attention to detail is second to none. I don't buy it."

"Either way," I try to drag him back into playing with the Play-Doh, "he's here with someone, so he's not worth thinking about."

I manage to convince Josh to drop it and we turn back to our creations until someone calls his name. A Daddy I've met before saunters over, barely says hi to me, then asks Josh if he's interested in 'doing a scene' with him. He might have just said "Hey, wanna fuck?" for all the good his attempt at subtlety does him. Josh bites his lip, clearly torn between wanting to blow off some steam with this guy or sticking with me.

"Go," I wave him off, "have fun. I'll text you tomorrow."

Josh wraps his arms around me in a grateful hug, wishes me a happy birthday one last time, then disappears into the crowd of caregivers and Littles, holding the random Daddy's hand. I drop my lump of Play-Doh with a sigh. It lands with a heavy splat on the table in front of me.

Happy birthday to me, indeed.

After scanning the space around me and not finding any

more familiar faces, I decide to throw in the towel. It hasn't been a bad night, but once again I'm heading home alone. Even a one-night stand would be welcome at this point, but it seems like I'm not even good enough for that anymore, either.

There's an ache in my chest that won't go away, and my vision blurs as I push to my feet and trudge towards the door on the far end of the room.

With my gaze directed to the floor, I'm so lost in my woeful thoughts that I bump into someone. "Damn, sorry." Mortification burns beneath my skin as I look up to properly apologize.

I don't recognize the Daddy I've bumped into, but I can read his expression very well as he looks me over and clearly finds me wanting. "Where's your Daddy?" he asks. His tone isn't particularly friendly.

Part of me wants to wave my wrist at him and tell him to learn the flags, because mine make it clear that I'm unattached, but I hold my tongue. I'm in the wrong here, after all. I wasn't looking, and I walked into him.

"I was just leaving. Sorry for bumping into you." Attempting to step around him, I'm surprised when he grabs my wrist.

I'm bigger than him, but I'm also pretty non-confrontational. Especially when I'm still coming out of my Little headspace and am admittedly already emotional.

"Someone needs to teach you to apologize properly," he says.

I blink, then shake myself. "Look, dude, I'm not in Littlespace right now. I'm actually just heading home and—"

"Too bad, boy. We're going to talk about this."

Is this guy for real?

I stare back at him, taking him in. He looks to be in his mid to late thirties. He's got slicked back, almost greasy looking blonde hair and pale skin, and his eyes are a cold blue color. He's at least half a foot shorter than me, and probably forty pounds lighter, but his grip on my wrist suggests that he's stronger than he looks.

I don't want to cause a scene, so I try again to defuse the situation. "Look, I'm sorry I wasn't paying attention and that I ran into you. Please let me go."

"Are you trying to tell me you're turning me down, boy?" He looks me over again, his lips curling. His Southern accent twangs with a sharpness that sours it for me, even though I'm normally all over a good, old-fashioned drawl. "You're, what, fifty? And huge. Littles like you don't get many prospects, and *you're* turning *me* down?"

Even though this guy is an absolute jackass, the appraisal hurts the same way it always does, and I was already emotional before this unexpected confrontation. My throat tightens, my eyes sting, and my skin burns as the humiliation rolls over me. "Please," I beg, my voice thick with unshed tears, "just...let me go."

The guy laughs in my face. My gut churns. "You gonna cry, boy? You think that's going to make you more appealing as a Little?"

"Red light," I croak, trying to step back, but he follows my movement, caging me in.

"We're not playing right now," he dismisses. "There's nothing to safe word out of."

He's making me feel small in all the wrong ways. I should be able to stand up for myself. I should be able to use my larger body to rear up and intimidate him. But he's pressed all the right buttons to make me forget that I'm capable of it.

My hands shake as tears finally spill down my cheeks, and I

close my eyes and beg for the ground to just open up and take me now.

"Back off," a new voice interjects, sounding beyond pissed off.

I open my eyes to watch as Hot Young Daddy slips himself neatly between my aggressor and me. It startles the other guy enough that he drops my wrist and I take an immediate step back, adding more distance.

"What the hell does this have to do with you?" my would-be tormentor demands.

Hot Young Daddy's shoulders are tense, but I can't see his face because he's facing the other guy and his back is to me. He still sounds furious as he answers, "He asked you to stop. He used his safe words. You need to back the fuck off."

Jackass —my new name for the asshole— scoffs and gestures at me over Hot Young Daddy's shoulder. "Just look at him. He wants the attention."

"*He safe worded.*" My rescuer repeats, beyond seething now. "Fuck off. Or do I need to use the house safe word and get the moderator involved?"

My eyes widen. That's not necessary at all. We don't need to make an even bigger scene here. I couldn't take the additional attention, and I certainly don't want to ruin anyone else's night. Using the house safe word is not a trivial thing. I should know: my company engineered the monitoring system.

"Pfft," Jackass leans around Hot Young Daddy and gives me another degrading glance over, "he ain't worth it." Then he turns on his heel and heads off into the crowd on the other side of the room.

My heart is hammering in my chest and I clench my hands into fists at my sides, willing them to stop shaking. I look at the ground again. I feel so stupid. How can I be this physically imposing, as no Daddy ever fails to remind me, and yet still need to be rescued? And I just let the asshole wander off where he might upset someone else. I'm a coward. Absolutely pathetic.

"Hey," Hot Young Daddy's voice is gentle now. Warm, if tentative. It's also much closer than I anticipated.

When I look back up, he's directly in front of me, his blue eyes lined with concern. He's even more attractive up close. I hate myself a little for thinking that.

"Are you okay?" he asks softly.

I nod, finding it too difficult to use my words.

He cautiously lifts a hand to my cheek and uses his thumb to wipe away the evidence of my tears. His touch sends tingles up my spine and I swallow convulsively.

"You sure?" he double checks, and I lament the loss of his touch as he pulls his hand away.

I finally find my voice, hoarse though it might be. "Yeah," I hesitate. "Thank you for stepping in." I'm man enough to admit that I needed the help, even if I should have been able to handle the situation myself.

I'm not the macho posturing type, the sort of man to argue that I had it covered when I clearly did not. That tends to surprise people, but not this guy. His eyes go all soft and understanding.

"You don't have to thank me, sweetheart."

Sweetheart. The endearment has my heart in my throat all over again. When was the last time anyone called me something so...so...affectionate? Oh, God, I'm going to cry all over again.

There's something seriously wrong with me.

"I'm London," he says, introducing himself while I struggle

to get my shit together, and then extends the same hand that was cradling my face only moments ago.

I accept the handshake. His hand is a little smaller than my own, his fingertips calloused where mine are smooth. I'm betting he works with his hands. He's got that rugged, outdoorsman look about him, even if he is clean shaven and wearing business attire.

It takes me a moment to realize that he's still waiting for me to speak. "Matteo." I don't know why I give him my proper name. I much prefer Matt or, when I'm little, Matty.

London opens his mouth to say something else, but a loud call of "Uncle London!" has him turning to face the new voice.

It's the Little in the Belle costume. She stomps up with a pout on her lips and barely glances my way. "You promised we'd dance again."

Instead of capitulating, London arches an eyebrow at her. "*Katie*," he says in an authoritative tone that has my dick twitching in interest, "you're being rude. I was talking to someone." Here, he gestures towards me, before telling her, "I know your Mommy wouldn't want to hear that you're going around interrupting conversations and being bratty."

Katie's eyes widen. "No. Don't tell Mommy. I'll be good." She turns to me and offers a sheepish grin. "Sorry. I just love dancing."

"Good girl," London praises, and fuck if I don't want him to call me 'good boy' in the same way.

She sticks out her hand and I'm quicker to shake hers than I was his. "I'm Katie."

"Matty," I answer, feeling myself relax back into my Littlespace to meet her at the same level. She's really cute: buxom and dark haired, with round cheeks dusted with bright pink rouge and matching glossy pink lips. Her hair's a bit messy from her prior exuberant dancing. "I like your dress. Belle's my favorite princess."

Her eyes light up and she starts tugging me towards the small dance floor. "Mine too! I want a library. *And* a talking teacup."

"I want a Beast." The confession slips out of my lips easily, and I feel myself blush at London's answering laugh.

Katie, thankfully, steamrolls the conversation forward. "What about a closet that can tell you what to wear and help you get dressed?"

"Or a kitchen that cooks for you."

She giggles and I realize too late that I'm in the middle of the dance floor with her. "I don't dance," I tell her, but she rolls her eyes.

"You do now, Matty."

At least when I'm in Littlespace, I'm not expected to have rhythm or moves. She takes my hands in hers and sways her ample hips from side to side, pulling me into following the motion.

We're halfway through *Under The Sea* when she leans towards me with a conspiratorial grin. "Uncle London *likes* you."

At my actual age, those words should not induce a swarm of butterflies in my belly, but they do. It takes all of my self-control to not turn and seek out the man in question with my eyes. Instead, I arch an eyebrow and wiggle my butt to the beat. Dancing this way has been surprisingly fun, and in my Littlespace I've been able to avoid worrying about looking ridiculous. My refutation, when it comes, is mild. "I'm too old for that to be true."

"*Pfft*," Katie does an uncoordinated spin, "he likes older men." Her expression turns a touch pensive. "But he's never been a

Daddy before."

I stumble over my feet. *"What?"*

She shrugs, as if the bomb she just dropped doesn't change *everything*. "He brought me tonight 'cos my Mommy had to work. He's not part of the whole…" she gestures wildly around the space, "…scene."

I can feel a part of me breaking at that. Clearly, despite my attempts to be rational, I'd started to hope that maybe I had forged some sort of connection with London. That maybe we could have had a fun night together, if not more than just that. But if he's not really a Daddy, even if he is kink-friendly enough to bring his friend here as a proxy caregiver for a night, I'm right back to where I started.

"Katie," London interrupts us, his tone back to that low, stern one that screams 'natural Daddy', but he's looking at me pointedly even while he addresses her. I don't know when he snuck up close enough to overhear our conversation, but I almost die when he adds, "I think that's something Matteo and I should discuss between us."

"Yes, Uncle London." Katie doesn't sound at all repentant. If anything, she looks pleased with herself.

I make a mental note to never introduce her to Josh.

London's lips curl with amusement, then he checks his watch. "It's getting late, kiddo. I promised your Mommy I'd bring you home before the spell wears off and your dress turns back into rags." The pout she wore earlier returns in full force, but before she can whine, he points his index finger at her. "No complaints or there'll be corner time."

For a guy who isn't a Daddy, he sure as fuck seems to know what he's doing.

Katie sighs and nods with resignation. "Yes, Uncle London."

"Good girl." London praises, then looks at me. "Where'd your friend go? Do you need a ride home, too?"

Josh drove us in, but with him otherwise occupied, my plan was to go get changed and order a Lyft. "I'm fine," I tell him, even though I really want to take him up on his offer. There's no point putting myself through that. In addition to me being far too old for him, he's not really a Daddy. I'd be setting myself up for disappointment.

"Not what I asked," he counters, pinning me with a knowing stare. I fight the urge to fidget under his gaze. "Do you have a ride?"

Willing my instant arousal to fuck right off, I shrug. "I'm going to order a Lyft."

London doesn't even hesitate. "Nope. You'll be waiting forever *and* will have to pay a premium for the neighborhood and peak rates. I'll drive you."

"And if I live on the other side of the city?"

His grin turns wolfish. "Then we'll have more time to talk."

Chapter Four — London

I t took all my self-control not to flatten the asshole who had harassed Matteo. For fuck's sake, the guy was getting off on making Matt cry. Where the room moderator was, or why nobody else around us had stepped in remains a mystery to me, even though the altercation was taking place off to the side of the room. It was clear as day that Matt was uncomfortable, and when I got close enough to hear him safe word only for him to be ignored, I'd snapped.

I might not be involved in the BDSM world, but I know enough to know that ignoring a safe word is like a cardinal sin.

I probably should have reported that asshole for it. Sadly, it's too late now.

But, oh, Matt is somehow both everything and nothing like I'd thought he'd be. He's tall —taller than me, and I'm not exactly short at 6 feet tall— and big and brawny. *Those arms...* I want to lick over the lines of his tattoos, tracing the ink that highlights those bulging muscles. But, even though his physical appearance is undeniably tough and hyper masculine, he's a soft, shy soul.

We make our way out of the epic playroom, travel back down to the main club floor via the elevator and then swing by the locker rooms so Matt can grab his things and get changed. I barely bite back the urge to ask him if he needs help: I've never helped Kate get changed before, so why would I ask this man I've only just met? Especially when it's clear that he's not in Littlespace anymore.

While Kate and I lean against the hallway wall, I feel her eyes studying me. "You really like him, don't you?"

"I only met him, like, an hour ago."

Her full lips twist into a wry, knowing smirk. "You've been sneaking glances at him all night."

She's more observant in her Littlespace than I gave her credit for.

"You've seen the man," I shrug, gesturing vaguely towards the locker room. "He's hot as fuck."

"You remember that I'm into women, right?"

I snort. "Doesn't mean you're unable to appreciate beauty in all its forms, male or female. I'm not saying you'd be attracted to him; I'm saying his hotness is obvious."

"Touché," Kate laughs. "You're really defensive about this guy. It's cute."

"I've been called a lot of things in my time, but 'cute' isn't one of them."

"Yeah, well, I've never seen you have zero chill around a guy before, either, so I guess it's all new territory."

"I have chill." Yep. That's my genius response. *I. Have. Chill.* Ugh.

It's Kate's turn to snort and she reaches up to pat my shoulder condescendingly. "Sure you do, London."

"Shut up." Oh, I am on fire tonight. So quick-witted. The amused sparkle in Kate's eye tells me her thoughts have gone the same way, but then her expression sobers.

"He's a Little," she says softly, and there's a world of subtext in the three words.

My sighed "Yeah" acknowledges it all.

I'm not a Daddy. I've never really considered being a Daddy. Outside of playing the Uncle London role with Kate, I've got zero experience with the kink or the lifestyle. So is being interested in a Little —even one as hot and intriguing as Matteo— really going to end well for either of us?

Also…just how little does he get? He wears a diaper, that much I could see, but does he *use* them? Kate wears them for the feel and aesthetic only —or, at least, that's as far as she goes around me— but I know that everyone's exploration of the kink is different.

Does he regress often or just occasionally for fun? Does he want a Daddy to take control of most of his day-to-day stuff, or does he just want a partner to play scenes with? From what I've observed of his personality, he's submissive, sensitive, and non-confrontational…and seems to soak up any affection or positive reinforcement like a sponge. I wouldn't be surprised if he's looking for a full-time Daddy.

Then there's the fact that he appears to be in his early forties and I'm not even thirty. Would he even want a Daddy so much younger than him?

Not that I am a Daddy.

Jesus, am I actually considering it?

When I'd overheard Kate telling him that I'm not a Daddy, my heart had seized. That was a conversation I had wanted to have with him. That, apparently, I *still* want to have with him.

But I have no idea what I want to say.

Kate's right: I *am* interested in him. More than I should be for having just met the guy. But everything about this is new to me and I don't know if the lifestyle is something I genuinely want or if I'm only now considering it because of my attraction to Matteo.

Could I be a Daddy? I mean really? Without it feeling weird?

Playing with Kate is always entertaining, but that's the extent of my experience. Sometimes I'll cut up her food or give her a bottle, but there's none of the other caregiver stuff between us. I'm the fun 'Uncle'. That's it.

And yet the thought of bathing Matteo, of dressing him, of being the person who kisses his boo-boos and looks after him…Well, it's oddly satisfying, and there's no hint of 'nah, too awkward for me' vibes at all. In fact, it sets off butterflies in my belly.

Huh. Who knew?

Kate's staring at me expectantly.

"What?" I ask.

"You're actually thinking about it, aren't you?"

There's no point denying it. Not if Matteo proves to be as interested in me as I am in him. "I am." I swallow, glancing over at the door to the locker room. "I guess I'm gonna need to talk to you and Cherie. Pick your brains on what, exactly, I'm thinking of getting myself into."

Kate's expression softens. "You're kind of a natural already, you know? As Uncle London, I mean. The Daddy vibes are pretty strong. You've got the voice and the instincts down pat. From there, it's just about finding what works for the two of you…and having fun with it." She waggles her eyebrows and pitches her voice low for the last bit.

Matt strides out of the change room before I can reply, and I almost swallow my tongue. He's wearing painted-on dark wash jeans and a tight black polo shirt which emphasize his strong thighs and bulging biceps respectively. He's got a black duffel bag slung over his shoulder, which I assume contains the onesie he'd been wearing earlier. To look at him now, you'd never know the guy was a Little, or that he was at all sweet and submissive.

"Yeah, okay," Kate huffs and nudges me, murmuring, "you were right. I'm gay, not blind."

I chuckle and a feeling of warmth sweeps over me as Matteo's expression flits between Kate and I, his insecurity painted on his handsome face. "What'd I miss?"

"Nothing important," I'm sure to keep my voice light and even, then I gesture in the vague direction of the exit. "Shall we?"

Anywhere else, I'd say we would have made a strange looking group: the big, tattooed guy, me in dress pants and a button down, and Kate in her costume. But nobody gives us a second glance as we head back out of the main doors and into the stark foyer.

"Oh! Matt!" We all turn as the woman behind the reception desk comes around it. She heads towards Matteo and wraps her arms around his waist, her head barely coming to his shoulders. "Happy birthday. I should have said it when you came in, but—"

"Josh is a distraction," he chuckles. "Sorry about him."

The woman pokes him in the chest with her index finger, "That boy is not your responsibility. He's been giving me grief longer than you've been a member." There's a fondness in her voice that belies the complaint. "Still, I hope you've had a good night?"

"Yeah," he scratches the back of his neck, suddenly realizing that he has an audience. His cheeks flush.

Her eyes widen as she takes me and Kate in, and then her lips pull into a knowing grin when she addresses him again. "Making new friends?"

"*Meg,*" he says in warning.

She laughs and pushes him back towards us, making a shooing motion. "The night's still young. Go enjoy your birthday some more."

"So…" I grin as we step out into the cool night air. "Birthday, huh?"

It's only as I ask that I recall his friend, Josh, saying something about it when I was eavesdropping earlier.

Matteo looks distinctly uncomfortable. "Yeah."

The smile slips from my face when I do the math and realize that he'd clearly arrived with a friend (under duress, if the conversation I'd overheard was any indication) who had then disappeared and left him on his own. *On his birthday.* That doesn't sit right with me. Still, I don't know what to say to make it better.

Thankfully, Kate steps in. "Have you had cake? I maintain that it's not a real birthday without cake."

Matteo shakes his head. "Nah. No cake. I haven't really been in a celebrating mood for the last couple of birthdays." Then, as if he's ashamed of having brought the mood down, he forces a bright smile that doesn't quite meet his eyes and jokes, "I'm getting old. Losing count and shit."

Alarms blare in the back of my brain. *He's hurting.* He might be trying to cover it up, but there's pain in his eyes and something about the tense set of his shoulders has me wanting to wrap him in my arms and never let him go. I can't imagine

38

why his friend would have left him like this. On his actual birthday, no less.

I know I should let it go myself, but I can't see that happening. Someone needs to look after this man.

"Please, you're, what, forty?" Kate asks, brazen as always.

"You're my new favorite," he points at her, then upturns his palm and makes a 'gimme' gesture, curling his fingers back towards himself a few times. "Keep the flattery coming."

She pushes, "There's no way you're much older than that."

"You're not subtle, you know that?" He might be calling her out, but he's grinning so her tactics appear to be working. "Forty-fucking-five, if you absolutely have to know."

Kate's gasp is over-the-top dramatic, but that's Kate for you. "No! You lie!"

"I wish."

"Okay," I intervene, chuckling at their antics as I fish my keys from my pocket. We've been walking towards the car, parked in the designated lot behind the warehouse. I click the button to unlock it and the orange lights flash twice in the darkness. The lot is lit by a couple of large floodlights, but it's not super bright. "Here we are."

"Matteo can ride shotgun," Kate declares, gathering up layers of tulle and satin in preparation of smooshing herself into the back of my Hyundai. "It's your birthday," she tells him when he moves to argue, "and you're taller than me. Your legs will thank you for it. Besides, London will drop me off first, so it saves you having to get out at my place."

He can't fault her logic, so he thanks her. Then, hesitantly, he says, "It's Matt."

She stares at him quizzically.

"I prefer Matt. Only my dad ever called me Matteo."

Past tense, I note. This guy's been through some shit, I can just tell.

"Noted," I acknowledge easily, and we all climb into our seats.

Kate keeps conversation flowing from her spot in the middle of the backseats, talking about how fun the night was and thanking me again for stepping in for Cherie. Then she explains to Matteo (*Matt*, I correct myself mentally) that her wife is her Mommy and was called into work last minute. Matt makes appropriate comments of commiseration, and then they compare notes about their favorite activities of the evening. By the time we pull up outside Kate and Cherie's place, the pair have exchanged numbers.

"You should totally come for a playdate," she demands of the big man, stars in her eyes at the thought. "I don't have many Little friends. We, uh, we don't get to socialize very often."

My heart squeezes for her and Cherie, and I'm once again filled with the feeling that the latter desperately needs to find a new job.

Matt smiles a sad smile at her. "I, um…I'm stopping the Little stuff," he says, full of apology and a jumble of emotions I can't pinpoint. "Tonight was a last hurrah, I guess."

"You…*what*?" Kate's frozen, her leg suspended out of the open car door, her bafflement palpable. "You can't just turn off your kinks, Matt. If being a Little makes you half as happy and relaxed as it does me, you're going to be miserable."

"I'm alr—" He stops himself abruptly, but I fill in the rest in my head.

Already miserable.

Oof, my heart.

Kate doesn't miss it, either. Her eyes fill with compassion, then flit to me for a second before she says, "Just please think

40

about it, Matt. You might find joy in it again." Yeah, she's really not subtle, but I kind of love her for that. Her attention turns back to me, clearly giving Matt a chance to process. "Thanks for tonight, Uncle London." Then, quieter, "Take care of him."

After I've watched her safely enter the building, I start the car again. The silence between Matt and me is awkward, and I hate that.

"So..." I start, wondering where my usual charisma has gone. I've always considered myself a natural conversationalist but, with this man, I feel tongue-tied and off my game.

"I appreciate you giving me a ride home."

Ugh. Strained small talk. I don't want this at all. I want the spark of connection we had in the club. I want to hold him and call him sweetheart again, because the way his eyes had lit up at the simple endearment was pure magic. I want to try things with him I've never done before. I want to see him smile and laugh again. I want to know what his lips feel like, what his tongue tastes like, what that scruffy beard feels like against my skin.

Jesus Christ, I've known him for barely a couple of hours and I'm infatuated.

He startles when I reach out and grab his hand, but he doesn't disengage from my hold. "Here's the thing," I tell him as I pull away from the curb, "I'm into you."

I feel him tense. "You're, what, twenty-five?"

"Twenty-six," like the extra year makes any difference, "but is that a deal-breaker?"

"You're not a Daddy."

I have to tread *so* carefully here. I'm not pointing out that only minutes ago he said he was giving up the lifestyle, because it's obvious that it's a part of his identity. And the longing in his voice makes me want to offer him the world, but it's not that simple.

"No," I answer slowly, "but…I'm finding myself interested in trying."

Matt whips his head around to face me, but with my eyes on the road, I can't meet his gaze. From the corner of my eye, I can see that he studies me closely as he asks, "Why?"

I'm not going to tell him that it's just because I'm into him, because that sounds a little crazy even to me. And, having had a little bit of time for some introspection on the topic in the last hour or so, I can honestly say that it's *not* just about him.

"I've watched Kate and Cherie's dynamic for a few years now," I explain, "and what they have is special, y'know?" I give him a quick glance as we roll to a stop at a red light, exchanging soft, understanding smiles. "I'll admit that I've been curious, I guess, but never really motivated to head to the club to play with strangers. But tonight…" I swallow, drumming my fingers over the top of the steering wheel. "Tonight, when I saw you…when that asshole was giving you shit…something inside me *shifted* and I felt…" Like I *needed* to defend and protect him. To hold him. To kiss him and take his pain away. But I'm struggling to put those feelings into words.

He does it for me.

"Like a Daddy."

I can still feel his eyes on me after that quiet, but awe-filled assessment. My lips curl upwards. "Yeah," I nod.

We're both quiet for a few minutes after that, with Matt's directions to his place the only thing breaking the silence between us. It's not a tense silence, though. More contemplative than anything.

"You don't…" he starts, then stops. "Never mind."

"No, what?"

I shoot another quick look his way before setting my eyes back on the road. I'm still holding his hand, but he's fidgety.

I don't press him further, content to wait him out. After a little while longer, he asks, "You don't think I'm too old, or big, or tatted, or...or whatever? You know, to be a Little?"

He sounds so meek and pained as he asks the questions that I fight back the surge of anger at whoever has hurt him. Men like that absolute fuckweasel in the club. Men who don't deserve a second's thought, but who have obviously inflicted a lot of damage.

"Absolutely not," my response is firm and without hesitation. "You're hot as fuck, Matt. And you look fucking adorable in a onesie."

"I...*what?*" The disbelief in his tone is palpable.

Instead of giving in to the urge to pull over so I can lean across the center console and wrap him in a strong hug, I squeeze his hand as tightly as I can. "You heard me."

"Yeah, but..."

I stay silent, waiting for him to get his thoughts together.

It takes a bit longer this time before he sighs heavily. "My ex introduced me to age play," he begins, and it's not what I was expecting, not by a long shot. "I was in my early thirties. Nowhere near this bulky. Only a couple of tatts."

"Okay..."

Turning his head to look out the window, he continues, "Obviously, I loved it. It was...freeing, I guess, and it spoke to me like nothing else I'd ever experienced. And it worked well for us. We, uh, we were together for almost ten years."

Whoa. "That's impressive."

"Yeah, well, it felt less than impressive when he dumped me.

It felt more like a waste. Of my time, my youth, my..."

"Love?"

I catch his nod again out of the corner of my eye and give his hand another squeeze.

"I felt stupid. Especially because he was clear that, uh..."

Realization dawns. "He said you were too old and too buff." I frown. "But he was with you all that time."

"*Bingo.*" Matt sounds resigned. "All those years where he pretended to be into the changes I was making..."

"Yeah, but you did that for you, not for him."

"And fucked myself over."

"Why? Because a bunch of close-minded dickwads said you don't look the part? Last time I checked, it takes all sorts to make the world go around. *I* love seeing you little. There's something about the contrast of such a huge, alpha-looking kind of dude looking all soft and cute and cuddly." It's word vomit. A stream-of-consciousness ramble that bypasses my filter. I feel my own cheeks heat after the words register in my brain. "Sorry. That was too much."

"You really meant that." He says after a moment, clearly stunned.

My head bobs. "Confession time," I acknowledge lightly. "I *may* have a type."

"Let me guess," there's a confidence in his voice now that I haven't heard from him yet, and it sends a thrill of arousal straight through me. "Your type is huge, alpha-looking kind of dudes with unexpected soft sides who are old enough to actually be your father?"

There's nineteen years between us, so technically he's not wrong.

"What do you know?" I drawl, finally managing to summon

my usual flirtatious tone. "You got it in one."

Chapter Five – Matteo

"Would you, uh, like to come in?" I ask London when we pull up at my place. It's been too long since I brought someone home from the club, and we both know that I'm not asking him in just for coffee. But there's a part of me that wants to ask for more than just one night, too.

I have to smother those urges. I've always been the type to get ahead of myself, and tonight is proving to be no different.

Honestly, tonight has been surreal. This kid (this *man*, I correct myself) has been so unexpected. The things he said about his burgeoning interest in being a Daddy rattle around in my brain on repeat. I'm relieved he didn't say that it came on suddenly when he saw me, as powerful a rush as that would have given my ego. Sexual attraction to another person is not reason enough to throw yourself headfirst into a Daddy/Little relationship, right? I mean, okay, I got into it for Trent, but we'd already been together for a few months at that stage.

Anyway, that's not the point. And it's not like London said he wants a relationship, even if that's where my thoughts keep drifting.

Ugh. My brain is a mess. I went into the club tonight thinking that it was the end of that part of my life, and then London turned up and suddenly I have *hope*. It's a dangerous feeling.

What does it say about me that I'm allowing myself to get so invested after a few hours with the guy? A guy who is almost twenty years my junior, at that. Not that age should matter between consenting adults, but I feel a kind of skeevy lusting after him all the same. Not to mention asking him into my home, openly inviting him in for sex.

London turns off the ignition and looks me in the eye. His blue eyes are warm but assessing. "Is that what you want?"

Okay, so physically he might be in his mid-twenties, but he's got maturity in spades. That deep, firm Daddy voice of his is going to do me in, especially when it's apparent that he's not aware that he's doing it. It's just him.

Fuck, that's hot.

"Please," I answer with a nod, biting back the honorific that my brain already wants to tack on to the end.

I'm rewarded with a genuine smile and he reaches to un-buckle his seatbelt. "I'd love to come in, then."

Don't read too far into that, Brightman. Just enjoy it as a one-night club hook-up.

My place is a standard suburban, ranch-style family home. Brick and tile, single story, three bedrooms, two bathrooms and a large backyard. I've been slowly renovating it, making it a little less like the ode to the 80s it had been, but the carpets are still a gross beige color and the walls —a hideous shade of brown— could use a facelift, too.

I lead the way from the front door, past what was the 'formal' living room in my parents' day on the right, the smallest bedroom (which I converted into an office) on the left, and into the open living-dining-kitchen space. The floors here are tiled —big, gleaming white squares— and the kitchen is shiny with new cupboards and appliances.

"Coffee?" I ask my guest, gesturing for him to take a seat wherever he wants. "Or a beer?"

It's been so long since I've dated that I'm pretty sure I'm already fucking this up.

Not that this is a date.

Fuck.

"Coffee sounds good," he answers, his eyes slowly traveling the space as I wander into the kitchen proper. Instead of sitting down in the living area or at the dining table, he follows me and leans against the kitchen counter, watching as I set up the French press.

"You're a coffee snob, then?" he sounds amused. "No pod machine for you?"

I grin. "Guilty as charged." There's something satisfying in using high quality beans and controlling the depth and strength of your own brew. I turn to the fridge. "Are you a cream and sugar guy?"

"Nope. Black coffee all the way for me."

"Be still my heart."

Trent always insisted on flavored creamers which, as far as I'm concerned, destroys a perfectly good cup of coffee. Especially with the copious amounts he used to use, the heathen.

London's chuckle is as deep and rich as the beverage I'm brewing, and it takes me right out of my musings about my ex. "You take your coffee seriously. Noted."

"You're taking notes, huh?"

There's no sign of embarrassment on his face. Instead, he just gives me a cheeky smirk that gives me butterflies. "I'm a quick study."

Even though his words could be interpreted as arrogant or cocky, I can tell he's being playful. Well, mostly. There's a quiet confidence about him that makes me want all sorts of things I'm sure he's not ready for, or that he's not even into.

When we take our steaming mugs into the living area, I sit on the end seat of my large, cushy brown leather couch and London surprises me by taking the seat directly beside me. I expected him to leave the middle spot free. He leaves a little space between us, enough so he can bring his knee up onto the cushion and turn to face me, placing his mug on the coffee table in front of us.

I rack my brain to think of something to say, but the spicy scent of his cologne is a distraction, as is the proximity of his body to mine. I'm suddenly all too aware that we're alone together, both of us sober, both of us already having admitted an interest in the other...albeit an implied interest on my own part. Hell, he brought me home from a BDSM club and accepted my invitation inside.

We both know where this is going.

Butterflies take up residence in my belly.

His eyes seem to darken as he watches me, then he says, "Tell me about what you enjoy doing when you're little."

It takes a moment or two for the words to register through the lusty fog in my head. Of all the things he could have said, I wasn't anticipating that. "I...huh?"

London's smile is kind. "Like I said before, I'm into you. And you being little is a big part of that. But I don't have a lot of experience with the lifestyle so...tell me about your Little side."

He cocks his head. "I know about the onesie and the diaper," he's matter of fact, without a hint of judgment, "but what else do you enjoy?"

"Playing. Y'know: toys, hide 'n seek, make believe...Uh, I love story-time, especially with cuddles. And bath-time..." I clear my throat. "With or without, uh, 'grown up' touches."

The corner of his lips quirks upwards, but he doesn't react otherwise. "Uh huh. What about being looked after? What do you want from your Daddy?"

Fuck, even him saying the word —not calling himself Daddy, but just asking hypothetically— has my dick twitching. I swallow. "That's the main draw for me, to be honest. Being cared for, I mean."

"I figured as much," he acknowledges, still warm and kind, but there's additional heat in his gaze that I hope to God I'm not imagining. "But what does that look like to you?"

"Attention," I blurt, feeling pathetic as the admission escapes me. "Like...a lot. I'm...I've been alone for a while and I just—"

"Want to be someone's priority?"

It's as good a way to phrase it as any other. I nod. "Yeah. So, like, having Daddy take control at home, making my decisions for me, giving me rules and structure and schedules. Lots of affection and reassurance, because I'm, well, a needy little boy." I look down at my lap, picking at my cuticles.

An index finger lifts my chin. London's expression is still open and free of judgment when I'm forced to look at him. "What else?"

"Uh," my thoughts are a jumbled mess, that simple touch doing more to me than I can process, "So, I like it when Daddy does stuff for me. Cuts up my food. Makes sure I've been drinking my water and eating healthy. Orders for me at

50

restaurants…but not off the kids' menu. Uh, and I like it when he chooses my outfits and dresses me?"

"Why is that a question?"

My cheeks burn. "I don't know."

Except I do. I want to know his limits. How much of this would he actually be okay with? Because I'm willing to compromise on any of it. And there I go getting ahead of myself again. He's asking out of curiosity, not because he's decided to be my Daddy.

"*Matteo.*"

Fuck me, Daddy voice is back. I don't even hate the use of my full first name when it's said that way. In fact, it's more arousing than I could have imagined. Funny how I've never felt that way when Charlie does it, though.

"I just…can you tell me if something's too much?" I cringe even as I say it. "Not that…not that I'm just assuming you want to be my…that you're considering…"

Those blue eyes light with understanding. "Oh, sweetheart," he reaches out and pulls me in for a hug, running thick fingers through my hair, "I thought it was obvious. That's why I'm asking."

The hope I was trying to stomp down inside me breaks free, tendrils of it curling through my veins and into my heart and head, making me giddy. Could it be that he does want more than a one-night club hook-up? With me, of all people?

"You're not freaked out by this?"

"Not in the least. Honestly, I assumed most of it anyway, having seen Cherie and Kate's dynamic. But I know everyone's a bit different, so I just wanted to know what *you* want as a Little." He cocks his head. "The dressing thing…do you prefer diapers or training pants or—"

"You know more about this than you said you do." I cut in, pulling out of his embrace and settling back in my seat, facing him again. I realize how silly the sentence sounds once it's out, but London seems to understand my meaning.

"I did a bit of research back when Cherie first told me about her and Kate. I wanted to make sure I wasn't gonna put my foot in my mouth or be taken completely by surprise."

I wonder if there's more to it than that, but I accept the explanation readily enough.

Then he repeats the question about my preferences.

I sigh, feeling my cheeks heat even before I answer him. "I like the diaper. It…uh, it helps me sink deeper into Littlespace faster." Taking a steadying breath, I might as well go all in. "And the whole changing routine does that, too. Like being laid out and powdered and having it wrapped around me and secured…it's more intimate than just stepping into a pair of tight underwear, I guess."

"I can see that," London's voice is still steady and kind. "Do you use them? Or is it more a sensory thing for you?"

I wish I could get even a hint of his feelings on the topic. It's understandable that this is a hard limit for a lot of people, Littles and Daddies alike. For me, it's not a deal-breaker, though I won't lie and say that the level of trust and intimacy involved isn't heady, nor that being able to sink so deeply into Littlespace isn't incredibly freeing. Still, it's never been something I've indulged in often, either. Trent only went with it to humor me whenever I was incredibly stressed and needed the additional release, if you'll forgive the pun.

"Not for years, and never often. Usually only when I've been so stressed that I needed to go real deep into Littlespace." I eventually answer, studying him closely for any sign of discomfort, "But wetting isn't something I desperately need as part of my Little experience if it's a hard limit for my partner, and it's also not something I'm comfortable trying early on with a Daddy, either."

If he's relieved, or even disgusted, he doesn't show it. He just bobs his head. "That makes sense. And, honestly, I don't know that I'd be ready to jump straight into it from a Daddy perspective, either. I'd want a bit more practice with the diapering process first. For us both to be comfortable with each other. To trust each other implicitly."

My heart leaps into my throat. He seems so confident about this, even though it's all new to him. It's like he's made the decision to jump in feet first and that's that.

It's everything I've been wanting, that I've been dreaming of, for *years*. And now it's within my grasp and…I'm afraid. Afraid that I'm going to get attached too quickly. Afraid that he will hate it, though he obviously has every right to. Afraid it's not going to work out and that he has the potential to hurt me more than any of the jackasses in the clubs have, if only because my hopes are climbing too high now. But, mostly, I'm afraid that I won't recover if it doesn't work out.

"Hey, you're shaking," London's concerned now, reaching out for me again. I go willingly into another hug, tensing when he asks me to explain where my thoughts had gone.

This strange, almost instant connection I feel with him only serves to fuel my inner turmoil. It's ridiculous that I should feel so strongly after knowing the guy for barely a few hours. Am I so desperate for affection that I'm latching on to the first person to show me the kind of attention I've been yearning for for years? I don't want to use the guy. He's too good for that.

"*Matteo*." Damn it, I'm almost certain he knows exactly

what he's doing now, even if he didn't earlier. "Talk to me, sweetheart."

The dam bursts and my thoughts pour forth from my mouth, bypassing my filter entirely. There's no rhyme or reason to them. No order. I just blurt out all of my concerns, my fears, and my hopes in a barrage of rapid-fire statements.

Despite my embarrassment, I tell him about how badly I would love for him to try being my Daddy. About how much I miss having someone who understands my needs. About how I desperately want to find someone who genuinely cares and wants to look after me, and for whom, in turn, I can be a good boy. The best boy.

This rambles into my snowballing feelings of inadequacy. My voice shakes as I tell him about how lonely and utterly pathetic I've felt; the rejected boy, not good enough for any Daddy. Lastly, I go into how miserable I've been, knowing that it's the choices I've made which have made me so undesirable.

It's like the last two years' worth just explodes out of me. Even though I've vented to my friends, it's never been quite like this. I've always held back with them, not wanting to burden them or make them feel awkward. But with London, this veritable stranger, I let it all out.

I realize that unloading like this is the least sexy thing I could do when I originally invited the guy in for a hook-up, but there's no stopping the flow of words, and I find the entire experience cathartic.

London holds me through it, carding fingers through my hair and squeezing me reassuringly. He doesn't interrupt once. Occasionally, I feel him make a sound of commiseration or understanding, but it's not until I've said the last of it and have then reiterated that I don't want to use him simply because he's the only man to show me even a sliver of the kind of attention I crave that he finally says anything.

But what he says isn't anything I expected at all.

"Can I give you a bath?"

Chapter Six — London

❧

After his outpouring of information, I can see Matt is emotionally and physically exhausted. The poor guy has clearly been holding most of that in, struggling away on his own for the last couple of years. Oh, and then there's the fact that it's his fucking birthday and, if not for my being here with him, he'd be alone for it.

It tugs at my heart, making it squeeze painfully in my chest. I'm overwhelmed by the same feeling I had when that asshole in the club made him cry. This time, though, I *am* able to wrap my arms around him, offering him what comfort I can, but I want to take away his hurt. I want to make him smile. I want to look after him and cherish him and, well, be the Daddy he so clearly needs.

Sure, there's the slight complication that I've never been anyone's Daddy before, as well as the fact that I've kept my lingerie secret to myself, but instinct will assist with the former and I get the feeling the latter won't bother him too much. I mean, he's a forty-five-year-old man who wears diapers for fun: if anyone will understand me wanting to wear panties because they make me feel good, I think it'll be him.

But would he *mind* having a Daddy who indulges in what's traditionally seen as a more effeminate kink?

Considering how beefy he is, would he prefer his Daddy to be the same? I'm solidly built (no abs to speak of but no beer gut either, though I can't deny there's a little softness around my middle) with a frame that rivals his, even if I am a little shorter. As much as I hate labels, I fit that whole 'masculine' vibe. You know, aside from my penchant for satin and lace.

But I'm getting way ahead of myself right now. Something about Matt inspires that in me. His vulnerability calls to me in ways I can't quite put into words.

So, instead of reacting to any of his emotional outburst (as desperately as I might want to address his specific concerns about me or the spark between us), I ask to give him a bath.

He blinks at me. "A...bath?"

I know I could have picked a far less intimate activity —one not involving nudity— but we met at a BDSM club, for fuck's sake. I'm also pretty sure he invited me in for a hook-up anyway, and this entire discussion has been dancing around our mutual desires to explore our connection, for lack of a better word. Besides, he's emotionally worked up and a bath will be relaxing if nothing else.

I nod decisively. "A bath, yes."

"Like...as a Daddy?" His question is tentative and spoken so quietly that I have to strain to hear it. There's a world of emotion packed into those few words —hope, longing, disbelief— and I want nothing more than to reassure him.

"Yes. If you're okay with that."

Wide green eyes look at me with that same 'are you stupid'

expression Kate gave me earlier this evening. "I am *more* than okay with that."

Which is how I find myself standing next to a giant-ass bathtub in the master bathroom. Unlike most of the house, this space has clearly been renovated recently. The tiles are modern white subway tiles with glossy black accents. The shower, like the tub, is spacious enough to easily hold two adult bodies (even those as big as ours), and the toilet is positioned comfortably between the two, with a double vanity on the opposite wall.

I'd half expected to feel nervous for this moment, but a sense of how right this feels settles over me instead, and I'm calm and confident when I ask Matt if I can undress him.

"You really want to do this?" He double checks, even as he comes to stand in front of me while the tub fills. "This scene?"

I grin. "I really do." Excitement simmers beneath my skin. Not just at the prospect of getting him naked, even though my cock stirs valiantly at the thought, but excitement at seeing if the Daddy/boy dynamic will work for me.

For us.

"Safe words?" He prompts. "I usually use the stoplight system."

That much I had gathered at the club, but I nod. "Perfect."

Matt hesitates for barely a moment before he shakes out his shoulders and closes his eyes, exhaling with only a hint of shakiness. When he opens them again, he smiles, and it almost takes my breath away.

"Okay, sweetheart, arms up." My hands move to the hem of his polo shirt and I'm gentle as I pull it up and over his head. He's only a couple of inches taller than me, so it's not as awkward a maneuver as I'd anticipated.

I turn to toss the shirt at the hamper in the corner nearest to the bedroom and then allow my gaze to rake over his body. He's muscular and toned, no six-pack, but with definition beneath those big, sculpted pecs of his regardless. His olive skin is damn near flawless, and his chest hair is dark and silver streaked. It's not copious, stretching out across his pecs and thinning as it tapers down his abdomen and into his happy trail, creating a natural arrow towards his belly button and beyond.

"You are beautiful, sweet boy," I tell him after drinking him in, allowing my hands to coast over his broad shoulders and down his front, raking through the coarse hair on their journey to the waistband of his jeans.

"Thank you," he breathes, then hesitates.

I clear my throat. "You, uh, you can call me Daddy if you want to." Though I did read once that it's a title that has to be earned, so I quickly add, "Unless that's too much for now, or too fast." Suddenly, I'm not feeling as confident as I was only minutes ago. Have I fucked this up already? "It's just…I don't like 'Sir' or anything like that, so…I mean…Daddy or London are good for me."

Yep. I've ruined it. That has to be some sort of record, right? 'World's shortest stint as a Daddy' or something?

Surprising me, Matt seems to relax at my fumbling. He presses his forehead to mine and lets out a happy little sigh. "I want to call you Daddy."

It's like fireworks explode inside me. I feel lit up from the inside, elated and energized. I chuckle and can't resist pressing my lips to his in a short, chaste kiss which only makes the ecstatic buzz inside me last longer. "We probably should have discussed it before we started, huh?"

"Meh," Matt shrugs, then rubs his bearded cheek against my clean-shaven one, though he can probably feel the prickle of a day's worth of growth there now. "We can make it up as we go."

"I like the sound of that." The pressure is off that way. This is an agreement to learn and explore together. Even though he's got years of experience as a Little, I don't feel like he has any expectations on how we should interact with each other in these roles. It feels like a clean slate for both of us, and that seems to reset my confidence.

He wiggles his hips from side to side with growing impatience, and I laugh. "Okay, I get the hint."

He's not wearing a belt, so I pop the button above his fly and then unzip him, hooking my fingers into the waistband and then dropping to my knees to tug the thick denim down. His legs are just as I remember them from seeing him romping around in his onesie, strong thighs and calves covered by a light carpet of dark hair. But the bulge straining against the front of tight black boxer briefs —and currently at my eye level— draws my attention, even as I help him step out of his jeans, thankful that we'd both kicked our shoes and socks off earlier.

Staying in this position, I reach for the band of his underwear and look up at him. "Color?" my voice is tight.

"Green," Matt's reply is quick.

I pull his boxer briefs down slowly, watching his cock spring free. I practically salivate as I visually take him in. He's thick and long and gorgeous, with a bead of pearly liquid gathering at the tip of his purpling head as I watch.

Another conversation we did not have springs to mind as I contemplate leaning forward and licking that drop of precum off him. "Have you been tested recently?"

"Yes, Daddy." He sounds as affected as I am, and I can't even describe the reaction I feel to finally being called that name directly. It's like a bolt of lightning straight to my cock. I barely register that he's still talking. "Last week. Tests were negative, and I'm on PrEP. I can show y—"

"I trust you, sweetheart," I interrupt before indulging in the temptation in front of me, bringing my mouth to the crown of his cock. "And I'm the same." That's all I say before I give into the urge to I tease him, sucking the precum from him, and he proves to be delightfully responsive, sweet moans egging me on. "You taste so good."

So good, in fact, that I'm tempted to forget the bath plan and suck him dry, but I force myself to pull back and push myself back to my feet. I glance at the tub and decide it can still run for another minute or two.

Asking Matt to stay put, I stride over to the vanity and start opening the cupboards beneath the sink. I grin when I find what I'm looking for, pulling out a small basket of bath toys and a red loofah with a plastic Elmo head attached to it. There's also a bottle of baby wash, so I grab that, too.

Setting my collection down on the floor beside the tub, I unbutton the cuffs of my shirt and roll the sleeves to my elbows. Matt lets out a needy whimper, and I turn to watch his pupils dilating as he fixates on my forearms, then looks me over.

"Perfect, Daddy," he says when his gaze finally meets mine. His cheeks are flushed, his green eyes glazing over. "You look… *whoa.*"

I glance past him and into the mirror above the vanity, immediately understanding that the business pants in combination with the rolled-up sleeves of my button down really do work for the Daddy vibes. It wasn't intentional – I'd just gone directly to pick up Kate after I finished work. But I'm glad for the outfit choice now.

With a smile, I lean over the tub and turn off the faucet, dipping my hand through a mountain of bubbles to test the temperature of the water below.

I right myself and offer Matt my dry hand. "Alright, sweet boy, I'll help you in."

He climbs over and sinks into the welcoming warmth with a deep sigh.

I observe him for a quiet moment. With his eyes closed and bubbles caught in his beard, his vulnerability seems even more obvious, and my heart gives a funny squeeze. Was it really only a few hours ago that we met? It feels longer.

"Which is your favorite toy?" I ask him when his eyes drift open, possibly at sensing my stare.

"Um," he bites his lip, a gesture which should look strange on such a strong-looking man, but which I can only think of as adorable, "duckies, please Daddy. I have two."

It doesn't escape my notice that he uses the honorific every time he addresses me. I don't know if that's because it was a rule with his last Daddy, or if it's because it's been a while since he's had the chance to call anyone by the title, but if it makes him half as happy as it makes me, I'm more than glad for him to do so.

Digging through the basket of toys, I locate the two rubber ducks. One is your standard yellow rubber ducky. The other is pink with multi-colored polka dots. His eyes light up as I hand them over, and it's a joy to watch him dunking them beneath the bubbles, splashing about as he creates a story where the two ducks go adventuring together. When I pick up a toy frog and join in, he blinks back surprised tears that make me angry at all those other men all over again, but I have him giggling within minutes.

"Daddy, it's a frog, not a dragon," he declares when I, as the frog, attempt to hold the yellow duck prisoner in my tower of bubbles.

"This is a magical frog," I argue, "who can breathe fire."

Matt laughs and brandishes the other duck, waving him at me. "Then Sir Pinkie is a knight. And he's gonna beat your dragon frog and rescue Prince Quacker."

A dramatic fight scene ensues wherein, sure enough, the evil dragon frog is defeated by the pink duck, thereby allowing the prince to ride off into the sunset with the knight.

My shirt is damp, the remnants of dissolving bubbles and splashes of water soaking into my sleeves and chest, but it doesn't bother me at all. I wear the watermarks with pride, having genuinely enjoyed the imaginative play, and I reflect on that for a moment.

Should I have felt strange playing so childishly with another grown man? Especially one who was a stranger until a few hours ago? None of it felt awkward or forced. It felt natural. Just like it does when I'm playing with Kate when she's little. I take it as another sign that maybe I really am meant to be a Daddy and I just never realized it.

Speaking of...

"Alright, baby, the water's cooling down so let's get you all washed, okay?"

Matt bobs his head, still beaming at me. He's well and truly in Littlespace now, and I'm thrilled that this is something I've been able to give him, considering how hurt and lonely it sounds like he has been. With a generous squirt of the baby wash onto the Elmo loofah, I scrub gently over his muscular, tattooed arms first, then over his strong chest and down his stomach. The water is deep, so I ask him to stand so I can properly wash his lower body.

He's not hard anymore, but that cock of his is still impressive even like this. All I do is wash him, though, scrubbing the foaming soap over his thighs and calf muscles, then getting him to turn so I can do the backs of his legs and up to his perfect ass. I don't tease him here, either, as tempted as I am. It's not the right moment for it. Not this time, anyway. Having him sit back down, I go over the rippling muscles of his back and then rinse him off.

"Time to get out," I declare, smiling when he makes a sound of complaint. "We've gotta get you dry and dressed and, if you're good, I'll read you a bedtime story."

Once again, his eyes turn suspiciously moist, and he blinks rapidly to clear them. "Okay, Daddy."

I'm fairly certain that telling myself to be rational and take things slowly right now is pointless, because my heart lurches yet again. I can't quite explain it, but something about this man pulls me in like nobody else I've ever met. I want to take away his hurt and make his days brighter. I want to worship him and show him that he's worthy of affection and attention. I want to be his Daddy for more than just tonight, even if that means letting him in in a way I've never allowed anyone else, sharing my own secrets and hang-ups like he's been brave enough to do with me.

But the strangest thing is that that revelation doesn't scare me. It should. I should be slapping myself for jumping in so deep, so fast. For not even questioning these urges to explore completely new and insanely intimate experiences with a man I met only a handful of hours ago. And yet I'm at peace with how fast this is going. It feels *right*.

He might have only invited me inside with the intention of a single night of fun, but I think we both know this is going to be more than that. Just how much more, though, is yet to be seen.

I towel him dry and then lead him into his bedroom. Nothing about this space even hints that he's a Little. It's tastefully decorated with a king-sized bed decked out in a navy blue comforter and a couple of gray cushions. The bedside tables are plain and painted black, and I spy a matching chest of drawers through the open door of the walk-in robe.

"What do you like to sleep in, sweetheart?" I ask, already moving towards the walk-in robe as though I do this every night.

I push back the rising hope that we might get to that point sooner rather than later.

"Just loose boxer shorts," he answers. "Top left-hand drawer."

I don't know if the adult choice is his actual preference or if he's holding back for my benefit, but I don't push him. I select a pair of satin boxer shorts with an angry-looking cartoon squirrel emblazoned on the front, a pun about not touching his nuts printed on the right thigh. Matt chuckles when I hold them up.

"A gift from Josh," he explains, sounding fond and exasperated all at once.

"He sounds like a character." *Look at me not outwardly judging the guy for just abandoning his friend at the club on his birthday.* Not that I'm complaining about that too much – it led to me being able to hang out with Matt, after all. *Hmm, maybe I should thank this Josh guy...*

"He is."

I kneel in front of Matt and he places his hands on my shoulders, stepping into the shorts and allowing me to pull them up, standing back up along the way. Once I've made sure the waistband is sitting correctly and untwisted around his hips, I step back and look him over. "They suit you."

He grins at me. "Yeah, I kinda' love them."

I lead him to the bed and gesture for him to get in. "Do you have any storybooks?"

He briefly hesitates before he answers, "In the spare bedroom, three doors down the hallway on the left. There's a bookshelf... you'll find 'em."

I follow his instructions and find a room that is *much* more suited to a Little. The bed in here is twin-sized, the room itself much smaller than the master suite, and the bedding is super-hero themed. The promised bookshelf is stationed against the far wall, tucked into the corner. Next to it is a small desk with coloring books and crayons spread out across the surface. There are a few stuffed toys propped up against the pillows on the bed, and a wooden toy box at the foot of the bed which I discover contains blocks and a train set.

Having crossed the space to poke around, I look through the selection of books, all for children, and choose one titled *'Elmo's Circle of Friends'* with a grin. I'm guessing I know his favorite *Sesame Street* character for sure, now. I hold the book up for Matt's inspection when I return to the master bedroom.

He cocks his head at me when I ask him to scoot over. "Are you staying the night?"

Now the awkwardness which I should have felt before surfaces. Aside from the tiniest bit of attention paid to his cock earlier, we haven't engaged in anything sexual, not that I expected us to following his unleashing of emotion. And yet giving him a bath has felt even more personal than if we had.

We're in a strange sort of limbo right now.

"I didn't want to assume." But, oh, how I want to spend the night in his arms, or with him in mine…and I really do want more than just the one night if I'm being completely honest.

"I'd like it if you did, but I don't want you to feel, like, obligated or—"

I silence him with a kiss.

Chapter Seven — Matteo

London brings our lips together for the second time tonight. The first kiss was sweet, chaste and quick, but this one heats up quickly when I open my mouth to his, inviting his tongue to meet mine. We kiss slowly, exploring each other. His tongue is hot and sweet against mine, his lips just as soft as they look. When we finally pull apart, I can't help but let out a happy sigh.

"Mmm," he agrees.

"So…does that mean you're staying?" I feel ridiculous asking, like I'm a teenager again. I haven't felt this way about another man in over a decade. I'm giddy and a little nervous. Obviously, a large part of that is because tonight has been perfect. *He* has been perfect. I almost don't believe that he's never been a Daddy before.

He gives me a soft look and it gives me butterflies. "I'd love to."

"You can borrow a T-shirt and boxers if you want. Or sleep naked." I waggle my eyebrows at him.

"Don't tempt me," he laughs, the sound deep and rich, even as he wanders into my wardrobe. He returns wearing a plain black tee and a pair of loose cotton boxer shorts, the clothes he'd been wearing folded neatly over his arm. He hangs them over the armrest of the chair near the window, then slips into bed beside me with an endearingly unsure expression on his face.

"What?"

"You're out of Littlespace," he begins, then lifts the book he'd discarded on top of the covers earlier. "Should we maybe table this and talk?"

There's a part of me that wants to say no and demand my bedtime story and snuggles, but I push that down. Talking is more important. I basically unloaded on him earlier, and instead of addressing any of those issues, or potentially even to buy himself some time to think about them properly, we went straight into a pretty personal scene to test the waters of a Daddy/boy relationship. It's the strangest, most unexpected turn of events, but I have zero complaints about it.

"Can we still cuddle while we talk?"

Eyes lighting up, he opens his arms and I move into his embrace, rolled onto my side with my cheek pressed against his chest and his chin on the top of my head. It doesn't escape my notice that we seem to fit together perfectly like this, either. Like jigsaw pieces clicking into place.

"How did you feel about the bath?" London asks once I'm settled. Then he starts answering his own question, like he knows I need time to process my feelings.

I appreciate that more than he can know.

"From my perspective," he says, "I thought it went well. It felt good. *Natural.* I liked being your Daddy." He clears his throat.

"Did it help with your concerns? Or did it make them worse?"

"You're definitely a natural," I assure him, then realize that's not the part which is worrying him the most. I fight the urge to facepalm. "I'm less concerned now that you're not actually going to be into it."

His lips find my forehead, kissing it gently. "What about your fear that you're only going to get attached because I'm the first guy in a long time to do this with you?"

"You've proven me wrong on that front, too." I don't hesitate to answer.

From the second he started undressing me, that particular fear evaporated. I don't want him just because he's giving me what I crave. I want him for him.

I pull back a bit so I can look him in the eye. "I think the connection we've got, this...this *spark* between us...is real. We had genuine fun playing in the tub, right? And that kiss just before was so hot." Not to mention the way he'd sucked the crown of my dick for a few seconds before my bath. I understand why a blow job never materialized; we had to explore the Daddy dynamic first. And, now that we know that works, there's no reason to rush things.

Well, not unless this is just a one-night club hook-up type of thing for him after all.

My heart sinks at that thought, and I'm almost certain my expression mirrors my mounting worries.

"Hey, where'd you just go?"

"What do you want to get out of this?" I'm blurting the question before I can properly phrase it. "Because I don't think I can do casual, even if I thought I did when I asked you to come in tonight. I'm really an all-in kind of guy."

London's eyes are warm and his smile is fond. "I figured as

70

much. From what I've read, and what I've seen —and, hell, what I just experienced as well— this sort of thing involves trust and familiarity that a casual relationship isn't generally cut out for. Well, at least for most people. And, to be honest, I'm an all-in kind of guy, too. So..." There's vulnerability on his face again, reminding me that we're equals in this. It steadies my nerves. "I'd like to date you. Exclusively. To be your Daddy...if that's what you want."

"This isn't going too fast for you? Like, you're not just doing this for my benefit, right?"

I hate how insecure I sound.

Another fear is that he's just saying what I want to hear and then I won't hear from him again after tomorrow. But he honestly doesn't strike me as the type of guy to pull that sort of stunt. I can't know that for sure, but I want to give him the benefit of the doubt. I need to.

The covers rustle as he gets more comfortable, wriggling closer, pressing our bodies together. He's hard, his bulge grinding into mine, eliciting a soft gasp from my lips. "This is perfect, sweetheart. And I'm benefiting, too."

How can he possibly be so damn mature? When I was in my mid-twenties, I was a fucking mess. And that was *before* I discovered my kinky side.

I've got one arm trapped beneath him, but the other coasts down his strong back, sneaking under his shirt, teasing his skin before dipping towards the band of his borrowed boxers. He stills then exhales, "There's one more thing."

With our chests against each other, I can feel his heart rate picking up. Concerned, I pull my head back, watching him closely as I ask, "What's wrong?"

London swallows roughly, spots of pink on his cheeks. "I..."

He clears his throat but doesn't look away. "I like to wear lingerie. Namely panties. Lace and satin do it for me."

Huh. I wouldn't have picked that from his big, rugged frame. But now the image of him wearing a strap of lace and nothing else forms in my brain and my cock gets impossibly harder. "That's fucking sexy."

"Really?" He sounds bewildered, like this was not the reaction he was expecting. I can't imagine why, considering I think my kink is even more taboo, socially speaking.

My fingers tease at the top of the boxers again. "Are you wearing a pair now?"

His resulting nod is slow and hesitant. Gone is the bold, confident man I've seen all evening, and in his place is someone wholly relatable.

"Can I see you?"

If I hadn't been so focused on him, I think I might have missed the panic on his face in the dim lighting. "I've never…" He trails off, averting his gaze.

"Never what?"

"I…I've kept it to myself." He bites his lip. "I've never let anyone else see me wearing them. I've never worn them if I even thought someone else might see them."

I blink, surprised by that. "Really?"

London bobs his head in affirmation, blushing in the dim lighting.

Holy shit.

Even though I've been enamored with his self-assurance until now, this vulnerability is somehow even sexier. The idea that he feels comfortable enough to share this secret of his with me, a veritable stranger, is heady. Maybe he sees it as a mutual thing, though, considering the way I spilled my own secrets to him earlier tonight.

"I'm the luckiest boy *ever*." I blurt, then realize that he hasn't actually agreed to show me. I rush to fix my presumption. "I mean, I will be when you're comfortable showing me. *If*. If you're comfortable. There's no pressure."

London's shoulders relax, the tension in his body fading while I babble. Then he's kissing me again, cutting off my ramble and rolling me onto my back. This kiss is even more intense than the last. It's sloppier, harder, less coordinated. London ruts against me, grinding his cock against mine while our tongues twist together. I pant into his mouth while I rock my hips up to meet his movements.

"Fuck me," I breathe, managing to get the thought out through the lust-induced fog in my brain. "Please, Daddy."

London groans, a deep sound full of pleasure that rockets straight through me. "God, hearing you call me Daddy is something else."

I don't need to beg him any further, though. He rolls off me, kneeling on the mattress to pull his borrowed shirt over his head, and I watch through hooded eyes as his thumbs tuck into to the waistband of his shorts. After taking a steadying breath, he pushes the cotton down where it catches around his thick thighs, revealing the black elastane and lace through which his cock is making a bid for freedom, straining against the fabric.

His blue eyes are pinned on me, watching me for my reaction. He has nothing to worry about, though. If anything, seeing him like this turns me on more. I lick my lips, reaching for him. My fingertips brush against the smooth, silky front which is edged by soft lace scallops. His dick jumps at the touch.

"Gorgeous," I murmur, palming him properly now through the material. There's a damp spot forming over the head of his cock, as though I needed any further proof of how much he's enjoying this. Thumbing over it, I relish in the sounds he's making.

"You're killing me, sweetheart," London says after allowing me to tease him for a while longer.

I'm aching and leaking precum in my own shorts, ignored by both of us to this point. "*Daddy*," I practically whine, and I can feel the jolt of arousal that shoots through his cock when I do. Grinning, I file that information away, beyond pleased to have proof that he really does enjoy it when I use the title on him.

Whatever lingering fear I harbored that he might just be playing along for my sake evaporates completely and I'm elated because my birthday wish seems to have come true. I've found a Daddy. A super hot Daddy, at that.

Oh, sure, we don't actually know each other, and the age gap isn't ideal, but those are issues to discuss later. For now, I just want to enjoy the moment. It's been far too long since I've been with another man, and even longer since I felt truly free to let go and be myself in bed.

But with London I don't feel any reason to hold back. I can call him Daddy. I can let him take control. He doesn't expect me to top, or to dominate, or to boss him around (not that I don't enjoy being a bossy bottom every now and again). London knows that I'm needy, that I'm starved for affection, that I want to be looked after and have my decisions made for me. And I trust him to give me what I need. I trust him when he says he wants more than just tonight.

Lunging, London rolls me onto my back again, kissing me while he struggles to push his shorts the rest of the way off. It's an awkward maneuver, but we're both worked up now and neither one of us has the capacity to be suave.

His hands tug at my boxers next, and I lift my hips, my mouth still connected to his, helping him remove them to a point where I can kick them free. I don't care where they land after that.

The only clothing separating us now are those sexy-as-hell panties he wears, and my hands slide over his perfect, firm ass, squeezing the smooth skin I find there. It turns out the pants are cut like cheeky boy shorts, the scalloped lace fanning out from his crack in graceful arches, feeling like they frame the globes of his cheeks to perfection. I want to demand that he stand up and show me, but that would involve stopping the kiss – not something I'm inclined to do.

"They're gonna have to come off if you want me to fuck you," London all but growls against my lips. I've been toying with the edges of the lace and squeezing his ass, so I'm not surprised that he's thinking along the same lines as I am.

"You strip, I'll grab the lube."

"I like the way you think."

We're a mess of limbs and movement for a brief interlude, each of us dedicated to our respective tasks, and when we meet back up in the middle of the bed again, there's no longer anything between us. He's gloriously naked and I drink in every inch of him, my hand gravitating to his hard length.

His cock is shorter than mine, but he's fucking thick. Just imagining the delicious stretch and burn of something that size inside me has me steadily leaking precum. The idea of him being inside me without even the thinnest barrier is even hotter.

"You sure you're good without a condom?" I double check. It was one thing to confirm we were both free of STIs before he licked my dick earlier, but this takes that implicit trust to a whole new level. I haven't gone bare since my relationship ended. But this thing between London and me isn't a one-night stand. It's the start of something new. Something serious. "We're going to be exclusive, right?" He'd said that earlier, hadn't he? Or am I just imagining the things I want to hear?

I feel only slightly awkward as I ask these questions, like a fumbling teenager instead of a grown man. But it's important that we're on the same page. Especially when we're talking about unprotected sex. I get tested regularly and I'm on PrEP, but you can never be too careful.

London nods. "Definitely exclusive, sweetheart." As if reading my thoughts, he adds, "Like I said before, my tests have been negative, I haven't been with anyone since my last test, and I'm also taking PrEP." His lips curl upwards and he bumps our noses together. "And I want to see my cum dripping out of your tight, little hole."

Holy fuck.

Yeah, I'm done talking.

I lunge for his mouth, pulling him against me until our bodies are flush against each other. Wriggling my hand between us, I wrap it around both our cocks as best I can, pumping them together with our combined precum aiding the glide of flesh against flesh. This kiss is rough and needy, and I can't distinguish which moans and groans belong to him, or which have come from me. His hands feel like they're everywhere, exploring my body, tugging at my hair, driving me crazy for him. Then he picks up the lube from where I dropped it at my side.

I spread my legs for London without instruction, far too desperate to make him work for it. I can feel him smiling into our kiss and hear the click of the bottle lid opening. He manages to work some lube onto his fingers in a one-handed movement that has to be well practiced, then snaps the lid shut again, dropping the bottle back where he found it before bringing his coated fingers to my hole, all without breaking our kiss.

He doesn't tease me or draw out the prep, something I'm grateful for in this moment. There'll be time for slow and romantic later. Tonight, we're both too wound up. I bear down as he's adding a third finger, already babbling obscenities and begging for his cock.

"Fuck me already," I demand in a flash of lucidity, "please, Daddy."

The magic words have him stroking more lube over his cock. We make matching sounds of pleasure as he notches the head against my entrance and slowly sinks in, stretching me further with short, careful thrusts until he bottoms out. He gives me a moment to adjust and, once I've relaxed properly and the burn is less pain and more bliss, he pulls back out and then thrusts back in again in one smooth move.

It's not long before we find our rhythm, London spread over me so we can kiss as feverishly as we're fucking. My hands grip his shoulder blades, slipping over sweat-slicked skin, and a gasp is torn from my lips as he grazes my prostate.

"*Daddy*," I plead, hoping he'll hit that same angle again.

"*Fuck*," he draws the word out, his voice thick and gravelly, "you feel so fucking good, sweetheart. So tight and hot for Daddy."

I almost come at that. If he thinks me calling him Daddy is hot, it's nothing on hearing him refer to himself that way. My hips rock upwards, out of sync, my cock seeking friction.

"Please," I'm back to babbled begging, my heart hammering

and my breath coming out in pants as the tension builds. I'm so fucking close, but I need more. "I need…" I don't know what I need. Not really. All I know is I'm cresting the wave, but my orgasm is just out of reach.

London shifts his weight onto his left arm, resting on his elbow and forearm so he can slip his right hand between our bodies. When his hand wraps around my leaking cock, I almost sob with relief. "Is this what you need, sweetheart?" He begins pumping me in time with his thrusts.

I don't answer. I'm unable to. Instead, I manage to partially warn, "I'm gonna—" My words cut off with a grunt as his dick pistons over my prostate again and I come hard, spurting over his hand and coating both our bellies.

He rides me through it, his movement becoming jerky before he curses and slams back in one last time, his hips stilling while the heat of his release fills me. When he pulls out slowly, I wince only a little. He presses a gentle kiss to my left pec, then flops onto his back at my side, catching his breath.

The silence between us is comfortable, but soon enough the sensation of his cum trickling out of me makes me squirm. London catches my movement and rolls out of bed, heading into the bathroom. I hear the cupboard open and shut, then the sound of running water. When he returns with a wet washcloth and cleans me up, my heart flutters.

It's a stupid thing to get emotional about, but he's the first man to ever do this for me. Trent would always insist we shower, and I'd be out of bed and dressing myself during condom disposal after any of my rare hook-ups. But this tender, sweet action from London feels like the most intimate thing we've done all night.

I barely register him tossing the cloth back through the

bathroom door, or manhandling me against the pillows, but I do pay attention to the soft kiss he delivers just behind my ear.

"Sleep, sweetheart," he says, spooned up against my back. My eyes grow heavy, as though following his instructions is instinctive.

Best. Birthday. Ever.

Chapter Eight – London

"I want *all* the details," Cherie demands when I answer her call.

It's been three days since I took Kate to Littles' Night. Three days since I met Matteo. Three days since I discovered that I'm not as impartial to the lifestyle as I'd assumed. Three little days…and my whole world has changed.

"Honestly, I'm surprised it's taken you this long to hound me," I tell her, knowing she can hear the smirk in my voice.

Matt and I have texted every day. At night, I call him and read him a bedtime story. We haven't seen each other in person, but our connection feels just as strong as it did when we met. And hearing him call me Daddy still never fails to send a thrill of emotions straight through me.

"That's because I was waiting for you to come to me, jackass," Cherie interrupts my thoughts. "Kate came home telling me that you found yourself a Little of your own. *That you're considering being a Daddy.* And I just assumed you'd come talk it through when you were ready."

I can hear the hurt behind her words. Becoming serious, I respond, "I was going to, Cher, I swear. But, not gonna lie: this Daddy thing hasn't been as complicated as I thought it would be. Like…it's just been easy, y'know? Instinctive? So, I didn't really have any questions or anything after all." And the ones I did have —the ones more specific to Daddy/Little boy play— Google has helped with. "And I know you've been swamped with work, so I was gonna wait until you were free to chat."

"Hmm."

"Hmm? What 'hmm'?"

I spin my chair around from my desk. I'm a landscaper by trade, but I work for a company that provides landscaping to large businesses and corporations —hospitals, schools, resorts, that sort of thing— and, more often than not, find myself seated at a desk sketching plans and working around budgets than toiling outside on a job site. Considering I majored in psychology, this was not where I saw myself when I graduated college. But my part-time college job as a laborer helping at sites turned into a full-time job, which turned into a promotion and…here I am.

I share my office with another guy, Tom, but today he's on site supervising one of his projects. Our two desks are pressed together in the middle of the room, surrounded by glass walls. Three of them look out into the other offices and reception area. There's also a boardroom three doors down, but the glass walls there are frosted. That's generally where we host pitch meetings for clients, as well as our monthly staff meetings.

The fourth wall is a window that looks out over the city. From where I sit, I have the perfect view of the manicured grounds of the local college. It serves as a reminder of how far I've come and how different life is to what I'd imagined for myself only a few years ago.

"I should have seen it earlier," Cherie muses, finally answering my question. I always allow her the time to think before she speaks, and she affords me the same courtesy. We're very similar, and we understand each other's limitations. This is why we work so well as friends. "That you're a Daddy, I mean."

"Oh?"

Her laughter is tinkling. "London, you've always been a natural with Kate. You barely even blinked when I told you what we were into. You just rolled with it."

"Yeah," I say, drawing out the word as if she's slow on the uptake, "because you're my best friend."

"It's more than that. It's always been more than that, now that I really think about it."

"Cher…"

"No," she cuts me off sharply, and I can picture her shaking her head. "None of my other friends outside of the lifestyle, or my family for that matter, really get it. But from the first time you saw Kate in Littlespace, you just went with it. Zero judgment, zero hesitation. You just called yourself Uncle London and stepped in as a caregiver. Hell, you even enjoyed it."

She's got me there. "I did. I do."

Playing with Katie was always something I had fun with, as though it filled a need I didn't know I had. And, obviously, it had scratched the itch enough to keep me from realizing that I was actually into the lifestyle itself. Until I met Matt.

Her exhale is heavy as it travels down the phone line. "So, all this time, you've been a Daddy and neither of us realized it."

"Honestly, Cher, I don't think I was ready to realize it."

"Not until you met someone worth stepping out of your

comfort zone for, anyway." Cherie's definitely got my number.

"Exactly."

"And this guy is worth it?" There's an edge to her voice again, a protective sort of bite that makes me smile.

I think of my big, buff, tattooed, bearded boy and my heart skips a beat. It's been three days, but I'm so fucking attached already, it's bizarre. But, strangely, I'm not panicked about that. This thing between him and me? It feels right in a way I can't put words to. Like we're two pieces of a puzzle that just fit. He's got the capacity to break me, but I'm more than aware of how fragile he is in return.

I think of the look in his eyes when I shared my own secret. Beneath the desire, I'd seen his understanding and his unwavering support. It should be weird that a complete stranger's acceptance had meant so much to me, but it had bolstered me, given me the courage to truly be myself with him, and it had been freeing in ways I've never experienced before.

I don't even hesitate with my reply. "He so is."

* * *

'Dinner at my place tonight?' Matt's message pops up on my phone screen just after lunch and my lips immediately pull into a wide smile. One of the guys on my crew arches an eyebrow and I shake my head at him. He'll probably give me shit later, but I don't care.

'What can I bring?'

The animated ellipsis pops up almost immediately, then disappears and reappears a couple of times. Finally, Matt's reply comes through. *'An overnight bag.'*

I chuckle, wondering just how much overthinking Matt did before he worked up the nerve to press send. My boy is one of the shy ones and I love to push the envelope with him. Getting Matt to blush and squirm is rapidly becoming one of my favorite things. I hope my flirtatious tone is conveyed in my next message back. *'Do you have plans for me, sweetheart?'*

'You don't have to stay over. I'm sorry if that was too forward.'

Smile slipping, I click on Matt's name and press the call button, bringing my phone to my ear. I step away from the guys working on my latest project (a community garden paid for by the local council) while I wait for Matt to pick up. When he does, I barely give him a chance to say hello before I launch into my gentle admonishment. "There's no such thing as too forward with me, baby."

All I can hear on the other end of the call is his soft breathing before Matt eventually admits, "I just don't want to come off too clingy."

"Oh, Matt," I sigh, having forgotten that he's been hurt to this extent. That other men have made him feel like his 'neediness' (his word, not mine) is something to apologize for, or to smother. But the thing is, I love being reminded of how much he wants me around. How much he desires my affection and my care. Honestly, I'm just as needy (for lack of a better word) as he is in this relationship. "You will never be too clingy for me, I promise."

Matt's response to my declaration is a dry, self-deprecating chuckle. "You say that now…" He lets the sentence hang.

It's only been four days since we met, since we fucked, since we agreed that he'd be my boy and I'd be his Daddy, but I'm already all in. If anything, I've been champing at the bit to spend more time with him, but I've been resolved to let him set the pace, knowing that he's got concerns of his own to work through first.

Then his words from that first night come back to me. He wanted a Daddy to take control, to make the decisions and allow him to relax. Maybe waiting was a mistake. Maybe he needed me to take control with this, too, and I failed at that.

Ugh. So much for 'I feel like a natural at this'.

"Okay, I'm pretty sure I've fucked up," I blurt out before I can think better of it.

"What? How?"

I wander further away from the guys, then lower my voice for additional privacy. I mightn't be ashamed of my proclivities, but I don't need to become water cooler gossip fodder. "I've been giving you space, I guess. Letting you set the pace because I know you were worried that you might just be getting over excited at the idea of having a Daddy again. And I know my age bothers you, too." He makes a sound of protest, but I steamroll right over it. "And that's all totally fair. But you said you wanted your Daddy to take control, right? And, well, I didn't do that, did I? I left the ball in your court, and I'm sorry."

There's a whoosh of air down the line, and it takes me a moment to realize that it's an exhalation of relief. I curse myself a little more for dropping the ball like this so early into our relationship, but Matt's words are reassuring. "You're new at this," he says, quiet but firm. "And we didn't exactly talk things through as much as we should have before we…" He stops and clears his throat, and I imagine spots of pink appearing on those sexy bearded cheeks of his.

"We're going to sit down and set rules tonight," I say definitively. "Proper negotiation. I want this to work so badly, Matt."

I barely manage to stop myself from telling him that I'm

crazy about him. It's been four days. We've seen each other in person once, and all other contact has been via text, calls and two Facetime sessions. As comfortable as I am with how quickly I've become attached, I don't want to sound like a raving lunatic.

"Yeah, I do, too." Am I imagining it, or does he sound as wistful as I feel?

"Good." There's not much else to say beyond that. Jake, one of the youngest guys on my crew, is waving from across the expanse of recently laid turf, trying to get my attention. I sigh. "I've gotta go, sweetheart. I'll see you tonight." Those words send sparks of anticipation shooting up my spine.

"I can't wait." I can hear the smile in his voice and I grin.

"Me either."

* * *

At five minutes to six, I park my car behind Matt's in his driveway. We live a twenty-minute drive apart when there's no traffic, but it came closer to forty tonight. I caught every red light, and it was rush hour. All I've thought about since we ended our call this afternoon is wrapping my sexy man in my arms and kissing him senseless.

Well, that's a lie. I've thought about taking things further after the kissing, too.

But we've got things to discuss first. Everything I've read (and re-read) about the lifestyle says that limits, rules and expectations need to be set in stone. I don't want to repeat my mistake. Matt is a grown man, but he's already told me that he wants (no, *needs*) a full-time Daddy. I'm up for the job, but I want us both on the same page about what that entails. I need to know exactly how much leeway he wants me to give him, if any.

When he opens the door, my breath catches in my throat. He's wearing business attire, which doesn't surprise me given that he works for a Fortune 500 company (even though he's adamant that as an electrical engineer he shouldn't have to dress in such a corporate fashion), and it looks like it's been tailored to his large, muscular frame, fitting him like a second skin. His hair is tamed with gel, and his beard, while still more beard than scruff, is trimmed neatly.

"Fuck me," I say by way of greeting, and his grin turns predatory.

"I'm sure we can arrange that one day."

Oh, fuck yes. I don't know where this confidence has come from, but I love it almost as much as I love his usual shyness and vulnerability.

I step into his personal space and wrap my free arm around his back, reaching up behind his head to guide him towards me so our lips can finally become reacquainted. I drop my overnight bag at our feet as he deepens the kiss so I can use that arm to pull him flush against me. I don't care that we're making out like teenagers in the open doorway of his house. I couldn't wait a second longer for this kiss.

When we finally part, both of us breathing heavily and readjusting ourselves with matching smirks, Matt steps aside and closes the door behind me. I leave my bag where it is, figuring I'll grab it later, and follow him into the kitchen-dining-living area, which smells amazing and I tell him so.

"It's just pulled pork," he says, lifting the lid off a crockpot and stirring the mixture inside. "I've got some slaw and fresh burger buns. Figured it was nice and easy."

"It sounds awesome," I insist.

"It's still got a little more to go," he adds some extra seasoning and barbecue sauce to the mix and then puts the lid back on. He turns to smile at me. "Did you want a drink?"

"I'm good for now." Now that it appears he's not cooking, I close the space between us again, wrapping my arms around him. He sinks into my embrace and rests his head on my shoulder. "I've missed you."

"Mmm," he agrees, "me too."

I can sense his exhaustion and, even though I know we need to talk, instinct drives me to say, "Let's get you changed into something more comfortable. Okay, sweet boy?"

Instead of waiting for his response, I lead him by the hand to the spare room which contains all his Little paraphernalia. There's a dresser against the wall to my left, across from the bed, and I release Matt's hand so I can rifle through it. I dig out a set of pjs covered in cartoon ducks, and then open another drawer to find training pants. My hand hovers over them for a moment before I shake my head and open the next drawer down.

Bingo.

Pulling a diaper from the packet, I turn to face Matt with my selection on display. The minute widening of his eyes is the only sign of his surprise. "Color?"

It takes him half a second to understand what I'm asking. "Green." He cocks his head at me, then jerks his chin at the diaper. "Color?"

"Green." I appreciate that he's checking in with me, too. He knows this is new for me and, as confident as I like to pretend I am, we both know that it's a big leap into Daddy play. I smile and wave towards the bed. "Let's get you changed, huh?"

We move over to the bed and I drop the clothes I've chosen for him on top of the covers. He allows me to unbutton his shirt and tug it loose from his pants, helping to slip it off once I've pushed the sleeves back over his shoulders. His belt goes next, then I divest him of his pants and underwear.

"Let's get the shirt on first, then you can climb up on the bed for me, yeah?"

As soon as I help him get the cotton t-shirt over his head, I can see the change in him. He's not little, but he's immediately more relaxed.

Landing a gentle love tap to his perfect bare ass, I direct him to lie back across the mattress and then reach for the diaper, unfolding it and turning it into the direction I need. "Butt up, baby," I instruct, and he complies, creating a bridge with his body, his strong thigh muscles emphasized by this position. "You're gorgeous," I can't help but tell him, delighting in the flush that creeps over his skin. I slide the diaper underneath him and, when I'm happy that it's positioned where I need it, I get him to drop his ass back down, legs spread and bent at the knees. His cock is at half-mast, but this isn't about sex right now, so I ignore it, even though my own fills at the sight.

Ignoring my arousal, I ask, "I know you're not planning on using this," I tap the open diaper, making it crinkle dully. It's like a mixture of cotton and plastic, which makes sense to me, considering its purpose, "but do you want a barrier cream, or some powder? The whole changing experience?"

"Someone's been reading up," he teases, and I grin unabashedly.

"Damn straight." We'll talk about this soon, but I want to do everything right. So, yeah, I have been doing some research on the stuff I've got zero practical experience with.

Matt's smile turns soft and understanding. He wriggles his hips. "Powder would be great. I don't know if it actually helps, but I like to think it prevents chafing." He gestures to the dresser. "Top right-hand drawer."

I find the bottle of baby powder exactly where he said it was and return to my task. Pulling the front up and closing the sticky tabs is a simple enough process, and it's not long before I'm getting him to lift his hips again so I can tug his pajama bottoms up over his adorably padded butt.

"Better?" I ask, offering him both hands to pull him up from his reclined position.

He beams at me, the expression lighting up his face. "So much better. Thank you, Daddy."

I can't resist kissing him. I don't think that urge is ever going to disappear.

Chapter Nine — Matteo

Just over three weeks later, barring a few little stumbles due to miscommunication in those first few days, my relationship with London seems to barrel along with ease. He spends every second night at my place, and we've gotten into a proper routine. I indulge in Little time after dinner on those nights, and I've become used to sleeping with him spooned against my back. It's crazy to think that I was miserable and lonely a month ago. It feels like a different time entirely.

A knock on my front door has me frowning. I'm not expecting London this evening, or any deliveries come to think of it. When I swing the timber aside, Ash and Josh push their way past me.

"Hello," I greet sarcastically, turning to follow them down the short hallway after shutting the door in their wake, "how are you? Please, make yourselves at home."

"This is a welfare check," Ash declares, dropping down on my couch and arching an eyebrow at me. "You've been M.I.A since before your birthday, and you've only been dropping emojis in the group chat. No words," he emphasizes and points at me sternly, "*just* emojis."

Alright, I'll admit it: that's not really like me. It's not like my responses are usually long and flowery, but I've been distracted.

Feeling slightly miffed that it has taken my friends close to a month to notice my withdrawal, though, I fold my arms defensively. "I've been busy."

I feel marginally guilty for being combative, but I do feel a bit like they could have made an effort with me, too. I know it's a two-way street, but they knew I was struggling.

Then again, they both work full-time (and Josh, like his older brother was, is a cop, so his schedule can be unpredictable), and I *had* asked them to give me space.

Josh looks like he wants to argue, but Ash puts his hand on his soon-to-be brother-in-law's arm and shakes his head. Then he turns to me, empathetic but firm. "You asked us to back off. We gave you a month." His expression softens. "We were worried, Matt. And I miss our playdates. Don't you miss your Little time?"

More guilt begins to creep into my gut, and I fight back a blush. London's told his friends and family about me. I even met his Mom via Facetime last week, which went surprisingly well considering she's only a few years older than me. However, I've kept him a secret from my friends. Not intentionally, mind you. But I haven't gone out of my way to casually drop his existence into the group chat, either. He hasn't pushed me to introduce him, but now I wonder if he's noticed that I've been keeping him all to myself. I make a note to talk to him about it. The last thing I want to do is hurt his feelings.

Swallowing, I look down at my socked feet and scuff my toe

over a mark on the tiles. "Uh…I've kinda been getting my Little time in at home." I really can't look at them. "With my new Daddy."

I'm significantly older than both these men, but right now I feel like an errant teenager caught fooling around with the boy next door.

There's a moment of stunned silence before both Ash and Josh start firing a jumble of questions at me. When I look up to interrupt and attempt to answer them, the hurt on Ash's face makes me feel even guiltier.

He's half my age but he's become my best friend and keeping this from him probably seems like a betrayal from his perspective.

"It's really new," I try to explain. "I mean, I only met him on my birthday—"

"I was *with you* on your birthday," Josh argues, sounding bewildered.

I shrug. "Until you left me on my own because you found someone to fuck." The words come out harsher than I intended, but it doesn't make them any less truthful.

Ash turns to Josh and smacks his bicep. Hard. *"Really?"*

"Ow!" Josh pouts and rubs at the site of impact. Then he has the grace to appear sheepish. "Look, that wasn't my best moment, but Matty said it was fine."

Ash hits him again, punctuating every word in his next sentence with a whack of his open palm. "It. Was. His. Birthday. You. Dick."

"I know! I'm sorry!" Josh holds his hands up in surrender.

With an exaggerated sigh, Ash turns back to me. "Okay, so I can understand why you'd be avoiding us, considering Captain Oblivious here totally didn't help matters, but this is the sort of news I want to celebrate with you." His gaze turns imploring. "I was afraid I was losing my playmate. My best friend."

Well, that hurts to think about. Ash didn't exactly have an easy start in the lifestyle, and he'd be just as lonely without the guys as I would. "Shit," I rub the spot between my eyes, wincing. "I'm sorry. I just got caught up in the honeymoon period, I guess."

I'd wanted to stay in my happy little bubble with London. Wanted to indulge in something that was just for me. But I could have done that while letting the guys know that I'd met someone. Hell, I should have said something, and then they wouldn't have been worried about me.

I watch as a slow, smug smile stretches Ash's lips. He shakes his head, his curls flopping into his eyes. He brushes them back with the side of his hand. "Honeymoon period, huh?" He makes a 'gimme' motion. "C'mon. Spill. I want to know about this guy."

I grab beers for the three of us and drop down in one of the armchairs kitty-corner to the couch after handing the guys their drinks. "His name is London," I start, then jut my chin at Josh. "The hot young Daddy who was there with the girl in the Belle costume."

Josh's brown eyes widen and then he hoots and leans over the arm of the couch with his hand raised for a high-five. "Damn," he whistles, "nice catch, my man."

Laughing, I slap his palm, because, yeah, London's definitely a catch. "I'm waiting for the other shoe to drop," I confess, then I lick my lips. "He's...well, he's perfect for me." Even with the age gap, but I don't mention this to them. They're not going to judge me for dating someone their age.

"You've got me at a disadvantage here," Ash complains,

"because I wasn't there, and I have no idea who this guy is." He scowls. "Stupid Charlie scheduling meetings on your birthday."

"You should have let Ted bring you," Josh rolls his eyes. "Or Chance. Or even Spence."

Ash starts listing reasons this was impossible by counting fingers. "Ted had a date, Chance was out of town, and Spence had a late recording session." He fidgets in his seat. "And you know I'm not used to being little in public without a caregiver. I'm just not comfortable with that."

Josh has the grace to appear both apologetic and understanding. He gentles his tone and reaches out to squeeze Ash's shoulder. "I know, I'm sorry."

Ash waves the apology off. "It's fine. But I need to know *everything* about this 'hot young Daddy.'" He waggles his brows and pulls out his phone. "What's his last name? I'm gonna Facebook stalk him."

"Don't be stupid," I tug my own phone from my pocket. There's a text from London waiting on the screen and I swipe it away before I open my photos app and turn the screen to face my friends. "Here."

Ash grabs for it, closely inspecting the selfie I took on my last date with London. "Wow," he says after a moment, "you weren't exaggerating. Look at that jawline."

"Like Charlie's isn't just as pretty," I tease, and Josh scoffs. "I'm prettier."

Josh and Charlie look so similar that I honestly can't agree with him or deny it. Thankfully, Ash just shoves Josh and tells him to fuck off. He hands my phone back to me and probes for more information. "Okay, so his name is London and he's hot. I feel like there's more to him than that?"

It's not hard for me to take the bait, and I spend a few more minutes telling them about how we met (Ash hits Josh again when I describe the creep London rescued me from, blaming him for having left me alone) and giving a brief summary of our relationship to date. We've gone out a few times, but generally spend time here at my place.

I've been over to his apartment twice, but it's spartan and doesn't really lend itself to my Little time, so we've mostly hung out here at home. I get the feeling he likes it better here anyway. And it turns out that he shares my love of gaming, too, so when I'm not little —and we're not otherwise indisposed— we're playing *WoW* or shooting up zombies together. We share an easy camaraderie which makes it feel like we've been together for longer than just a month.

When my phone rings, I belatedly remember the message I ignored in preference of calming the guys down. I cringe and answer London's call, much to Ash and Josh's combined amusement. "Hi, Daddy," I say sweetly. I'm not above a little emotional manipulation to save myself from getting in trouble.

He's onto me, though. Sounding amused, he replies, "Hi, sweetheart." He pauses for a moment, and I ignore the guys leaning closer, trying to listen in. They're worse than a pair of sixteen-year-old girls, literally hanging onto the edge of their seats for gossip material. "Did you get my message?"

It sounds like he's driving, the echo of the call telling me that he's got me on speaker through the Bluetooth connection to his stereo, and I check my watch, knowing that he's been working late at the office recently. "I saw it, but Ash and Josh are here so I haven't had a chance to read it."

"Ah, that makes sense then." I can't quite read his tone. Then he sighs. "I got off early today, so I texted to see if you minded me coming over, but—"

"No! No buts, I mean." I interrupt, wanting to facepalm when I realize that he might think I'm telling him not to come. "Please come over." Across from me, my friends sit up straighter, grinning and nodding. "The guys wanna meet you anyway, and…" I feel my cheeks heat, "I miss you."

Which is ridiculous. I saw him this morning because he stayed the night last night. However, I'm still in that honeymoon phase of our relationship where I want all the time with him I can get. Even if it means subjecting him to the Spanish Inquisition by way of two of my closest friends.

"I miss you too, sweetheart," he says, his tone warm and relaxed again. "I'm about ten minutes away. I'll see you soon."

Ash and Josh race to the door like the overgrown toddlers they are as soon as London knocks. He knows it's unlocked and that he can let himself in, but he never does. I loiter in the hallway and clear my throat, waiting for them to move aside so he can come in. They have the grace to appear sheepish, but it doesn't prevent them from eyeing my boyfriend with open curiosity.

London takes it in stride, chuckling and greeting them with an outstretched hand. "You must be Ash," he turns to my best friend, shaking his hand first, then to Josh. His smile doesn't seem as warm as he steps towards the cop, even though his tone hasn't changed as they shake hands, "And the infamous Josh."

"Fair warning," I inform him as I accept my greeting kiss, "Ash got on the group chat and now the whole gang's on their way. So, you know, brace yourself for the interrogation."

"Charlie's just getting out of a meeting with some city planners and the guys who own The Grove, though, so he'll be a bit late." Ash laments as he tucks his phone back into his hip pocket.

"City planners?" London asks as we make our way back into the main living area. He takes my favorite armchair and pulls me onto his lap, which probably looks silly considering we're both big, bulky men. Still, I relax against him, and he rests his chin on my shoulder.

Ash is busy explaining Charlie's desire to build some community spaces and resources specifically for people in the BDSM lifestyle who need help. Ash was one of those people once upon a time, and if I hadn't had my dad to come home to after my breakup, I would have been, too.

With the arm wrapped around my waist, London gives me a knowing squeeze. "That's such a commendable project," he tells Ash. "The company I work for provides large—scale landscaping solutions for businesses and stuff. Maybe I can talk to them about whether we can help out?"

"I'm sure Charlie would appreciate that," Ash grins.

Josh derails the conversation, barreling in without any tact. Classic Josh. "So, London, how come we've never seen you at The Grove before? You new to town? Or do you usually go to one of the lesser clubs?"

"Actually, I'm new to the lifestyle," London answers easily. "My friends are in a Mommy/Little girl relationship, but until I stepped in for Cherie as a favor, I never considered how good a fit it would be for me."

"Wait, hold up," Josh is gaping at us now, his eyes darting from mine to London's and back, before fixing on London's firmly. His expression becomes hard. Protective. "Is this experimentation for you?"

"For fuck's sake," I huff at the same time as London calmly answers, "Absolutely not."

Then he quietly admonishes me for cussing.

His arm squeezes me tightly again, and I can feel him tensing. Before I can tell Josh to back off, though, my boyfriend's tone turns saccharine sweet. "I should probably thank you, though. If you hadn't abandoned Matt, I probably wouldn't have met him or realized how much I enjoy being a Daddy. His Daddy, actually."

"I didn't *abandon* him," Josh bites back, defensive and snarkier than usual. "He's a grown-ass man. He's twenty years older than you and me, my dude. He can handle himself just fine."

Ash intervenes, smacking Josh just as he had earlier. "Except it was his birthday, we all knew he wasn't in a great place emotionally or mentally, and Matt told us that the only reason he and London even got to talking was because some other asswipe was getting in his face, which wouldn't have happened *if you'd been there.*"

"Ah, so Josh is getting himself in trouble again, there's a surprise," Chance observes as he and Ted casually saunter into the room. Unlike London, they have no qualms just letting themselves into my house. To be honest, I don't usually have an issue with it. But, now that I'm seeing someone, maybe I need to set boundaries. I wouldn't want them to walk in on something private, after all.

Or I could just start locking the front door like a normal person.

Chance is a pretty affable guy. He's in his late thirties and, like Asher, has never been a gym rat. He's confident in his dad bod, scruffy reddish beard and near buzz cut, and more power to him for that. Ted is about my age and also happens to be Ash's boss – a senior partner at a local law firm. He's got a real silver fox vibe about him, and I think he looks kind of like

George Clooney, with his brown hair liberally streaked with gray, and his athletic build still well kept. They're both wearing jeans and t-shirts: not a surprise in Chance's case, but Ted usually appears at our get-togethers in a suit on a worknight. I suppose that he might have gone to the gym or something after work, but it still takes me a minute to process the unexpected outfit.

"Fuck you," Josh rolls his eyes, but he's smirking at our friends. Then he addresses Ash with a sigh. "But, yeah, okay, you're right. I messed up. I'm sorry."

"Apologize to Matt, dumbass, not me."

I flick a hand in the air to prevent Josh from doing that before I make the introductions between the newcomers and London. "Chance and Ted, this is London Hayes. London, these are my friends, Chance Baker and Ted Masters." I don't get off London's lap, though, so he's left to just nod at the guys, and they chuckle and nod back.

"Forgive me," Ted says, dragging one of the dining chairs out into the living room and situating it between the couch and the armchair London and I have commandeered, "but you're not at all what I expected when Ash said Matt had a new Daddy."

"Ted…" I growl in warning.

He laughs, all blinding white teeth and knowing eyes. As far as I'm aware, he never told anyone about the time I asked him if he'd be interested in being my Daddy not long after I was first introduced to the group and I'm grateful for that.

It was only awkward for a little while, and he was very kind about explaining, as most Daddies had, that I wasn't his type. To be honest, I don't think it would have worked out even if he had been interested. He's too polished, and our personalities would have clashed as Daddy and boy. I much prefer him as a friend.

With hands up in surrender, Ted shakes his head. "It's just an observation, Matt."

"Is it the age thing?" London asks in a neutral tone. "Or does my boy have a type I'm not aware of?"

"Mostly the age thing," Ted answers easily. He shrugs. "However, Matt's never brought anyone new into the group, so I'll admit that I've made assumptions where I probably shouldn't have."

"You think?" I scoff.

"Aww, c'mon, Matt," Chance has dropped into the armchair at my other side, "you're such a private person. I don't think I've even seen you little more than a handful of times, and you never talk about what kind of Daddies you're into."

I can feel my cheeks burning again.

Why did I ever think introducing them all to London was a good idea?

Chapter Ten – London

I can feel Matt getting increasingly more agitated with his friends and their not-at-all subtle probing as the conversation continues. They seem like nice enough guys, even if I still resent Josh for the way he'd treated Matt on his birthday, regardless of the fact that I probably wouldn't be with Matt if he hadn't been left alone.

Matt's best friend, Ash, is a couple of years younger than me, but it's obvious that he cares a lot about my boy, and that makes me appreciate him even more for it. And, when Ash's fiancé, Charlie, turns up, I find myself easily drawn into conversation with the guy. He looks a lot like Josh, which isn't a surprise as they're brothers, but is older and gives off a much more authoritative vibe.

"Charlie was also a cop," Matt explains as if he's reading my mind, "but…" He trails off uncertainly.

Charlie gives him a crooked smile. He's sitting on the couch and has Ash in his lap, a mirror image of me and Matt. I know they're also in a Daddy/Little relationship, and that Charlie has stood in as a caregiver for Matt over the last couple of years so the two Littles could have playdates. It's obvious that he also genuinely cares about Matt, and I don't know how to express gratitude for that. He finishes Matt's story for him with an easy shrug. "But a GSW brought an early end to my career, and now I'm trying to get some new businesses off the ground."

"Yikes," I blink, having been unaware of that. "That sounds like some scary shit. But Ash was telling me about the kind of community hub you want to get up and running, and I'm kind of in awe of that." I repeat my offer to see if the company I work for can assist with any landscaping needs. We probably can't do it for free, but maybe we could offer some sort of price cut. Hell, I'm even happy to sketch up plans and do a budget for them in my down time.

While Charlie and I chat about that, Matt relaxes back into me some more. I had been beginning to worry that he was keeping me separate from his friends for some reason, but I realize now that it wasn't a conscious act on his part. His friends are a big, boisterous bunch: all nosy and more than happy to intrude into Matt's personal life without shame. The last of the crew, a guy named Spencer, joins us just as talk of ordering pizza starts up.

Spencer and I receive a hasty introduction and he makes no secret of the way he eyes me up and down. He's tall and lean, his skin pale and a mop of wild dark brown hair atop his head. At a guess, I'd say he's in his late thirties or early forties, and the rectangular, wire-rimmed glasses framing his gray-blue eyes suit him well.

"I'll be damned," he says to Matt, "I didn't take you for the cradle robbing type."

"Why's our age gap any different to yours and Emma's?" Matt

challenges, and I watch a flash of hurt cross Spencer's face.

"Considering she left me," the other man grits out, "I wouldn't say using her and me as an example helps you here, man."

I bristle at this conversation. Spencer is the second of Matt's Daddy friends to raise these concerns directly in front of me. That said, I suppose I prefer them to be open about it than try to railroad him behind my back. At least Ted was kinder about it, though.

"I'm an adult and this dynamic works for us. If he doesn't mind that I'm twenty years his junior, that's all that matters to me." Offering the guy what I hope is an understanding smile, I add, "But I'm glad you guys care about him and aren't afraid to show it." Macho posturing drives me a little bit nuts, but none of these guys seem to be the type for it. Not even Josh, even if he does seem a bit bratty. Or maybe that's me projecting again.

Spencer stares me down for another moment before he grins and offers me a fist to bump. "You're gonna fit in just fine," he decides.

Matt snorts.

* * *

After ordering —and eating— enough pizzas to feed a small army, Matt's friends start ambling out of his house, each one of them patting me on the back and telling me they're happy that I'm a part of the group now. It's not lip service, either. They've already added me to their group chat and are treating me as though I've been one of them since the start. Ash and Charlie are the last to leave, and the former pulls me in for a hug.

"You're good for him," he says quietly, "I've never seen him so happy or relaxed." Stepping out of the quick embrace, he looks to Charlie, reaching to hold the other man's hand. He swings their clasped hands between them and begs, "Daddy, can we have a playdate soon?"

Charlie and I have already exchanged numbers and we agree readily. Matt nibbles his bottom lip. "Maybe we can invite Kate and Cherie, too?" He asks me. "I know Katie wishes she had more friends like me and Ash."

My heart swells. My precious, sweet boy. He seems to always be considering others and their needs. "I think that's a great idea, sweetheart." I wrap my arm around him and kiss his cheek. "We'll make it happen."

Charlie and Ash leave after exchanging final goodbyes and Matt and I are finally left alone. He hasn't had any time in Littlespace tonight and, even though he was with his friends, the change from routine is showing in the tense set of his shoulders. While he wouldn't have had supervised Little time tonight anyway, I know he would have spent some time coloring or playing with blocks on his own before I called to read him his bedtime story. He sags against me when I direct him to head to the bedroom, forgoing bath time.

I stop by the room I've dubbed his 'Little Room' and grab a set of pajamas with a teddy bear print, a diaper and the baby powder. His eyes light up when he joins me in the master bedroom and he sees the items in my hands.

"You're the best, Daddy," he declares, before his face slowly falls and he averts his gaze.

I'm on him in a second, lifting his chin gently. "What's wrong?"

"I...you're so good to me, so perfect, and I...I kept you a secret from my friends. Not because I was embarrassed or anything," the last bit is rushed out, and I know he's worried that he might have offended me, "but...I was being selfish. I didn't want to burst our bubble." His shoulders droop and he looks away, studying the wall. "It hurt Ash's feelings; I know that much."

A part of me is elated. Wanting to keep me all to himself is actually a very sweet motive. However, he's beating himself up right now, feeling guilty about upsetting his friend and also the possibility of offending me, and it hits me that this is one of those moments where I've got a choice to make.

When Matt and I first sat down and spoke about rules and limits, the topic of discipline was glossed over. He promised me that he wasn't a bratty boy, but that he would sometimes appreciate a spanking to get him out of his head. We haven't tried impact play for fun yet, but I can't help but think this is the sort of situation he meant during that discussion. Domestic discipline to settle him, not arouse him.

My instincts haven't let me down yet, so I bite the bullet.

"You're right," I tell him softly, but with an edge to my voice that has those beautiful eyes of his flicking straight back to meet mine. "Keeping information from your friends had the potential to hurt a lot of feelings, mine included. It didn't hurt mine," I add, reassuring him that we're okay, "but I can understand why Ash might be upset. And I'm proud of you for knowing that you made the mistake. But I think you need to feel consequences for this. Am I right?"

It takes Matt a moment to understand what I'm asking, and I help his thoughts along by resting my hand over the curve of his ass, patting him gently. The strips of skin visible over his cheekbones turn pink, but he nods. "Yes, Daddy. Please." He all but exhales the words.

"Good boy," I praise. While allowing that to sink in, I step towards the edge of the bed and sit down, tossing the things

I'd gathered earlier onto the mattress behind me. "Pants down, Matt. Then I want you over my lap."

He all but scrambles to obey, his slacks and underwear pooling around his ankles in record time. He kicks them off, sending them flying in the direction of the bathroom. Then he drapes himself over my lap and I take a moment to get him positioned so we're both more comfortable and that he's not going to put out his back.

I rub the perfect globes of his ass with my open palm. "After this, you're going to forgive yourself, okay? This is the consequence for your behavior. It's a clean slate after that. Do you understand?"

"Yes, Daddy."

I've never done this before, but I've done my research as thoroughly as I can. I'm not planning on going too hard on him, especially when I don't think he's done anything wrong. However, I can tell that he needs this and, after a month together without having to discipline him at all, even I feel like it's a necessity for us to experience this. Hell, maybe he needs it more often than I thought, but he doesn't know to ask for it.

Should he have to ask for it, though, or is it my job as his Daddy to know when he needs it?

I'm getting too lost in my thoughts.

"Color?" I check.

He doesn't hesitate, even if his back is ramrod straight. "Green."

After getting the circulation going beneath his skin, I pull back my hand and land the first slap. The skin meeting skin sounds out with a louder *crack* in the room than I'd expected. My palm stings with the impact, and I admire the pink outline

I've left behind on olive skin that's a few shades lighter than the rest of him. I deliver the next smack to the other cheek, then return to the first for the third.

Matt flinches after the fifth smack, the skin on his ass cheeks now red and tender, but his back is still rigid with tension. My aim is to see him let go, so I rain down a handful more swats until I see his shoulders shake and hear the first of his muted whimpers.

Even though I know this is supposed to happen, it hurts my heart to hear him upset. But this is just another facet of the Daddy role and, while it's not fun, I'll do what Matt needs me to.

I spank him a little longer and, once he's practically boneless and sobbing properly, I stop to rub gently over the heated flesh.

"That's it, sweetheart. Let it out." I pull him back up for a cuddle, holding him tightly as he cries into the crook of my neck. "You're such a good boy for Daddy, Matty."

He clutches at me and sobs harder. I'm not stupid enough to think that this is just about his conflicted feelings over not disclosing our relationship to his friends. He hasn't had a Daddy in years, and I have my suspicions that his last long-term relationship wasn't as balanced as it should have been. He's been deprived of proper care and nurture for too long, and I can only hope that I'm starting to fill that void for him.

As he starts to calm, I kiss his temple. "Let's get some lotion on that perfect ass of yours, get dressed and snuggle, yeah?"

Matt takes a shuddering breath before he nods. He's quiet through the aftercare — contemplative and boneless. But the tension he was carrying is gone and he seems genuinely relaxed, so I'm convinced I made the right decision.

Once we're in bed and he's clinging to me like a spider

monkey, he finally breaks his silence. "Thank you, Daddy," he murmurs into my chest. I rub my hand up and down his back soothingly. "I needed that. More than I realized."

"Mmm," I acknowledge sleepily. "Did you wanna talk about it?"

"Not really," he answers a few beats later. "I just...I..." A guttural sound of frustration travels up his chest and out of his throat. I wait, knowing that he's struggling to express himself. "It's been a while. A long while. I've always known that it helps me to work through my issues, in my own twisted way—"

"It's not twisted," I cut in, frowning. "It's a proven technique. I mean, I've read a bunch about spanking therapy online, and heaps of people find that it's useful to help process negative thoughts and emotions and stuff."

There's actually a whole lot of psychology behind it, which I found fascinating, but I don't bother going into that with Matt. That would derail the conversation and I can't risk that happening right now. Clearing my throat, I urge, "Anyway, you were saying?"

"I just didn't think it was going to feel like that," he admits. "Like...like I was drowning and finally coming up for air."

I card my fingers through his hair. "You probably had more stress to work through than you thought," I suggest slowly. "And maybe...maybe we need to talk about regular spankings to deal with that build up. Like...once a month?"

His index finger teases my nipple through the thin cotton of my t-shirt. "Could I still have sexy spankings, too?"

A smile stretches my face. That sounds much more enjoyable for both of us. "Of course, babe."

* * *

"So, you met the friends, huh?" Cherie grins at me from across the table. We're grabbing a bite to eat at a local café on our lunch breaks, which have miraculously aligned for once. She takes a delicate sip from her soda through the straw and then cocks her head. "Does this mean things are getting serious?"

Around us, there's a general buzz of conversations. The café itself is small, but bustling. We've nabbed a booth in the back of the space, and there are two others along this same wall, and three matching booths on the opposite side of the café. In the space in the middle, there are a few small, round tables and chair settings that barely seat two people each. It's busy enough that our conversation won't carry.

"Things have felt pretty serious since the start," I answer, scratching the back of my neck. "Which is new for me, I'll admit."

"It comes with the lifestyle." There's no teasing in her voice now. "Sure, there are some people who just enjoy the odd scene or two to scratch an itch, but most of us…" Bobbing her head from side to side, she searches for the best way to phrase her thoughts. "What we're doing is being really quite vulnerable with each other, right? We get that our kinks aren't exactly socially accepted, so to trust someone else to explore them with in depth is usually a serious thing."

Having taken the opportunity while she spoke to bite down into my chicken sandwich, I chew and swallow while I nod. "Yeah, that all makes a lot of sense. I mean, it's probably more acceptable for me, as a Daddy, to explore my kinks than for Matt, or even for you and Kate, but it's still one of those taboo things." I think of the chat I've been invited into (which I've had to mute because the guys talk a lot of shit) and smile. "But Matt's friends have welcomed me into their group and that's kinda' nice. I mean, we're all the same, y'know? So nothing's really taboo with them. We can just *be*." Then I realize who I'm talking to, and add, "Which we get when we hang out with you and Kate, too."

Cherie lifts her glass again, holding the straw in place between her index and middle fingers before she moves to wrap her bright red lips around it. "But it's different because they're Daddies and boys. They're more relatable."

"Well, Spencer's bi —his last relationship was with a woman— but...yeah." I frown down at my half-eaten meal. "It shouldn't make a difference, but it's still nice to talk to other men about this stuff."

"Hon, I get it. I'm not hurt that you want to talk to other Daddies for their perspective, too."

I really lucked out to have this woman as my best friend and I tell her so. "So, anyway," I shift the subject back, away from the unusual exchange of warm and fuzzy feelings, "Matt asked me to set up a playdate for him, Ash and Kate. You in?"

"Kate would love that," Cherie's face falls, "but with my schedule so up in the air, I've given up on trying to make plans."

"Seriously, you need to find another job."

She pushes her plate away and folds her arms over the Formica tabletop, then drops her forehead on top of them. Her voice is muffled when she laments, "I've been applying for *months*, London. Months, and not one interview."

It's rough seeing her like this, but I'd prefer her to vent her frustrations and reach out for help than bottle it all up inside. Unfortunately, I don't know what help I can offer her. "I know you don't have a lot of free time or personal time, but maybe you really should try to get your own business off the ground as a side hustle for now?" I suggest. "I still think there's a niche market for clothes and accessories for Littles who don't fit the standard mold." Kate and Matt are both great examples. "And I'd still happily be your partner in that sort of endeavor." I just have no idea where to start to try and get something like that off the ground.

Cherie sighs heavily and sits up, toying with the corner of her paper napkin. "It's a great idea in theory," she says, "but think of all the startup costs."

"We could take out a loan."

"Oh, *sure*," she stretches the word out with liberal sarcasm. "Imagine pitching that idea to the bank. 'Oh, hi, Mister Uptight Bank Lender Man, we'd like to start a business specifically to cater for plus-sized adults who like to dress as babies. Please give us all your money.' *Pfft.*" She scoffs after acting out her monologue. "Like anyone would take it seriously."

I laugh. "Well, not if you pitched it like that."

She balls the napkin up and throws it at me. It lands on my plate. "Okay," I hold my hands up in surrender, "let's table the golden business idea again for now and go back to my original question. Matt and I are both kinda' homebodies, so our weekends are always pretty free. So, how's about I call you on Saturday and see what your day looks like?"

And that's what we do.

Miraculously, Cherie and Kate have Saturday afternoon free when I call. Matt calls Ash and is ecstatic to discover that they, too, are available. He's practically bouncing off the walls by the time the first knock at the door sounds.

Today he's dressed in an adorable pair of footie pajamas, his perfect butt rounded with the additional padding of his diaper. His living room is already strewn with toys and blocks, brought out from his Little Room.

112

"I've never had playdates here," Matt explains as he grabs me by the hand and drags me to the front door, "I've only ever gone to Ash's house." He's sinking into Littlespace slowly, and I expect that's because he's not yet comfortable with Cherie and Kate. After today, I hope that changes.

I know my expression is indulgent when I reply, "Well, this'll be the first of many here, I'm sure."

He swings the front door wide open and, before I know it, turns shy, ducking behind me. Cherie grins at me, while Kate bounces on her heels at her side.

"Hi, Uncle London," Kate says excitedly, "we bought cupcakes! Mommy won't let me carry 'em, though." She pouts for only a moment before she leans over the threshold and sideways. "Hi, Matty!"

He's absolutely adorable, flushing pink and barely squeaking out his return greeting.

Ushering our guests into his home, I give him a squeeze. "Why don't you go show Katie around, sweetheart? I'm sure she's excited to see your train set."

Bless her, she plays along immediately, grabbing his hand and tugging him back through the house, chattering about how she can't wait to see what his toys are like. Cherie and I follow at a more sedate pace, sitting down on the couch and letting the other two do their thing. She seems a bit more relaxed than she did earlier in the week, the dark circles beneath her eyes no longer as noticeable.

We talk a little about how the rest of our respective weeks panned out, and then there's another knock at the door. One glance over at Matt and Kate, both focused on building a tower with the blocks, tells me neither has heard it, so I get up and let Charlie and Ash inside.

"The other two are playing with blocks right now," I tell Ash, who is dressed similarly to Matt, "so go nuts."

"Ugh, don't tell him that," Charlie jokes lightly as his fiancé scampers away, "or he'll wind up needing corner time."

From what I've seen of Ash, he looks like butter wouldn't melt in his mouth, but I wouldn't be surprised if he had a bratty streak. Thankfully, Matt does not. Which amuses me, considering his need for regular spankings and also his whole 'bad boy' aesthetic.

Still, I chuckle and introduce Charlie to Cherie. I travel back and forth between the kitchen and living room for a bit, bringing out coffees for us adults and sippy cups of juice for the Littles, then settle back into one of the two armchairs facing the couch.

Cherie and Charlie seem to be having an in-depth discussion about Charlie's plans for the kink community safe space and I don't want to interrupt. Instead, I watch the others as they play. Matt seems to have slipped comfortably into Littlespace, and the other two are right there with him. They each have a stuffed toy in hand and are enacting some sort of story. Kate's decided that Ash's stuffed penguin is the princess and that she and Matt, armed with a teddy bear and a plush sheep respectively, are on some sort of valiant quest to rescue the penguin.

"They're kind of adorable, huh?" Charlie asks, and it takes me a moment to work out that he's talking to me.

I tear my eyes away from the imaginative play and grin at him. "Every time I think 'this is it; he's reached peak cute Little-ness', I see him doing something new that's even cuter."

"And none of this is weird to you?" Charlie's gaze is sharp and assessing, even though his demeanor is relaxed. "Josh said you've never done the Daddy thing before. And, I'll admit, my own first Daddy-boy relationship was eye opening. It took me a while to get past some of my own prejudices, even though I was enjoying it…if that makes sense."

I shrug. "Honestly, if someone had told me that I'd be into this, even a few months ago, I might have laughed it off as not my thing." I shoot an apologetic glance in Cherie's direction. "Like, I've never judged anyone for it. To each their own and whatever. But, yeah, the concept itself does come off a bit…" I trail off, not actually wanting to label it negatively. Clearing my throat, I shake my head. "Still, living it feels as natural as breathing."

Charlie nods, scratching his stubbled chin as his expression becomes speculative. "Have you struggled with any of it? Like…for me, I never really got the bottles of milk thing when I started out. Weird, right? Totally down with the diapers and even the pacifiers, but I could *not* wrap my head around bottles." He chuckles, the sound pleasant and a little self-deprecating. "I'm good with them now, but it took a while."

"It was discipline for me," Cherie pipes in, gently placing her half-drunk coffee down on the coffee table in front of the couch. She leans forward around Charlie so she can address the both of us. "It took me a while to understand that, even though Kate's a grown woman, when she's in Littlespace she needs the rules and the consequences just as much as she needs the fun and the comfort." She wrinkles her nose. "Spanking's a hard limit for me, so we do corner time and writing lines, mainly."

"I haven't really come up against anything yet," I shrug. "Maybe because I'd already seen so much of what to anticipate when I spent time with you and Kate," I gesture towards Cherie, "and I didn't really have any ideas or expectations going into this? I don't know. I mean, it's not like we've tried it all yet. And, sure, it took me some trial and error at the beginning to work out exactly how much control he needed me to take but, even then, I wouldn't say it was a struggle."

"Huh," Charlie sits back. "Well," he says after a long moment, "if that changes, any of us are more than willing to talk it out with you. Ted was kind of my mentor when I first joined the scene."

"I appreciate that. And, hey, maybe that's something your community center can look into arranging? Like...Q&A sessions, or mentorships, or stuff like that?"

"The Grove already has something similar in place for Doms in training," Charlie muses, "but not so much for Daddies who Daddies who don't really consider themselves Doms in the traditional senses. At least, not that I know of." Cocking his head, he stares off into space. "Considering how much Ted helped me, I think it's a great idea."

The three of us talk about it some more, with Cherie adding in her thoughts about the pros and cons of Q&A sessions open to all walks of the BDSM lifestyle verse niche sessions. It's so good to see her putting her analytic mind and planning skills to work with such enthusiasm. I stow my observations away in my brain, but once the center is up and running, I make a note to suggest that she ask Charlie for a job there. She'd enjoy it a hell of a lot more than working for her piece of shit politician guy.

"Mommy," Kate interrupts the conversation a little while later, jiggling in a tell-tale way that has me hiding my smile behind my hand, "I've gotta go potty."

I give Cherie and Kate directions to the bathroom and catch the curious expression on Matt's face before he schools it.

I make another mental note to discuss that with him later. For now, I'm content to let him enjoy his playdate.

Chapter Eleven — Matteo

"Today was the best day ever," I declare long after our guests have left. I'm still coming out of Littlespace, riding the wave of endorphins from a very successful playdate – the first I've had with my Daddy supervising me. It's also the first I've ever hosted in my own home.

The whole experience seems to have cemented how real this all is, and I can't help but think that even when I was with Trent, it was something I was missing.

Daddy's lips curl upwards and he leans across the kitchen bench, where he's currently cutting up veggies for a stir-fry, to kiss me chastely. "I'm glad, sweetheart."

"Did you have fun with Ash's Daddy and Katie's Mommy?"

"I did," his voice is filled with fond amusement. "It was good to see them getting along, too."

"Mmm," I agree, nodding. "Charlie added them to the group chat."

London looks up from slicing a bell pepper, his eyes bright and happy. "That's awesome. They don't really get to socialize much."

"I know," my own face falls a little. "Katie's a bit lonely, I think." It's something I can relate to. Not all that long ago, that loneliness was suffocating, and I had friends to talk to at the time. She seems a bit isolated and that tugs at my heartstrings. I know she and Cherie have London, and he's wonderful, but bringing them in to our rag-tag group means giving them some additional emotional support, which is never a bad thing.

"I'm going to try and convince Cherie to work with Charlie, once his community center is up and running," London tells me after a beat. "I'm sure Charlie would benefit from that, too."

"And it would mean more regular hours and less stress for Cherie."

It's actually kind of genius. I can't see Charlie having an issue with it, especially not now that she's officially part of the group, even if she hasn't met the other guys yet.

We continue to chat about the afternoon just gone, with London more than happy to let me give him a play-by-play of my activities. He doesn't seem to mind, even though he was sitting in the same room for the entire experience and my stories aren't exactly riveting. Nevertheless, he smiles and asks questions and I'm filled with warmth I've never really felt before.

"So," he says when we're at the dining table, steaming bowls of veggies, meat and rice in front of us, "I noticed that you seemed *interested*—" he draws the word out carefully "—when Kate asked Cherie for help in the bathroom." He picks up his fork and digs into his dish with a forced nonchalance that has me cocking my head. After he chews and swallows his first bite, he asks, "Wanna talk about that?"

No longer in Littlespace, I take my own bite of the meal he

just prepared, barely stifling a moan as the flavorsome sauce hits my tongue. It buys me some time to get my thoughts in order. "It's, um, it's not something I've ever done with a Daddy," I eventually tell him.

"But you'd like to?" As usual, there's zero judgment or expectation in his voice or on his handsome face. There's also no hint of his interest, or disinterest, either. Still, without knowing where his thoughts are at, I'm uncomfortable discussing it.

I shrug. "Look, I've done the diaper wetting thing..."

"*Matteo*," Daddy-voice comes out in force in response to my dismissive, vaguely defensive attitude. He softens when I look up and across the table at him. "We're talking about two different situations. Sure, there's an element of embarrassment and trust inherent in both, but asking Daddy to help you pee is different to being changed."

I deflate. "I know," I sigh. "I'm just...I'm aware that it's a lot, you know? You've taken all of this—" I wave my hand around, trying to encapsulate the entire lifestyle "—in stride, but I'm worried that something like that is going to be too far out of your comfort zone. Too much, too fast."

Setting his fork down, London frowns. "We have safe words, Matt. They're not just for you. If I'm not comfortable, I'll use them."

"But..."

He sits back in his seat now, and I can tell I've offended him. "Don't you trust me to be honest with you?" When I don't refute the accusation immediately, hurt flashes across his face before his expression falls. "I see."

"It's not that I don't trust that you're being honest," I rush to try and fix my faux pas, pushing my bowl aside so I can lean across the table and reach for his hand. He lets me take it in mine, which is a relief. "This is all going so quickly between us, and I guess I'm still waiting for the other shoe to drop. You're kind of perfect, London. I don't want to jeopardize what we have. And I'm...I'm afraid that if I push you too far...if I make you safe word..." I look down, my throat suddenly tight. I can't even say it.

His hand squeezes mine. "You think that if I safe word, I won't be as into you anymore."

I tremble at the very suggestion but bob my head, still unable to look at him.

He lets out a breath and pulls his hand out from mine and my heart thuds hard in my chest. Then I hear his chair scraping back against the tile. I'm aware of him rounding the table and dropping into the seat beside me before he pulls me against him, holding me in a tight hug. "That's not going to happen, sweetheart," he murmurs, kissing the top of my head. "If I ask you to try something new and you safe word because it's not working for you, would you think less of me for suggesting the experience?"

Understanding dawns inside me and I feel stupid. "No."

"So why would you assume I would reject you in the case of my having to safe word out because I don't like the new experience?"

"I don't know."

He's silent for a moment, and I breathe in the spicy scent of his cologne. "I think you do," he tells me quietly.

I gnaw on my bottom lip. I'm terrified of rejection, that's hardly a secret. And from the very start of this, I told him all my concerns about a potential relationship between us. "I suppose part of me still thinks I'm not good enough for you."

London's body tenses and he hugs me tighter. "I don't know

how to convince you that you're wrong. But, if it helps, I sometimes doubt that I'm good enough for you, too."

"Wait," I sit up straighter, twisting in my chair to look at him in surprise, "what?"

He rolls his eyes, but a smile tugs at his lips. His hand comes up to cup my bearded jaw, his thumb smoothing over the strip of skin of my cheekbone, just beneath my eye. "You're fucking hot, Matt. You're also successful, own your own home and are super sweet. And I'm a lot younger than you. I'm barely starting out in my career. I rent a crappy little apartment, drive a shitty little car..." he huffs out a breath that could almost be a short laugh, "and I wear lingerie. Pretty sure it looks ridiculous on a body like mine. I'm hardly a catch for a man like you."

Blinking, I struggle to process his words. "You're not serious." London stays silent. "You're also fucking hot," I dispute his logic, ignoring his muttered admonishment about my cussing despite the fact that he started it, "and you've gone from a laborer to a planner in, what, a couple of years? So you're successful in my opinion. Not that it matters where you are in your career. Not to me. Your age means jack shit to me, too, and—"

"Seriously, Matt, language," he interrupts again, but with enough amusement that I know I'm still safe from punishment.

"And," I continue on as though he didn't cut me off, "I don't care where you're living as long as it's safe. Besides, the only reason I own this place is because my dad left it to me. I didn't make great life choices before Trent dumped me, y'know?"

I shake my head, realizing that I'm getting off topic before I continue, "Not the point." Now I let my hands slide down his sides, my thumbs tucking into the waistband of his jeans, teasing the silky material they find underneath the denim.

"Finally, I *love* your panties. Just thinking about you in them gets me all hot and bothered. And if you wanted to try out camisoles or corsets or negligees or whatever—" grabbing his hand, I place it right over my hardening cock which is pushing against the cargo shorts I changed into after our friends left earlier "—*this* is exactly what I think about that."

His fingers tighten over my erection, an almost inaudible groan issuing from his lips. "Yeah?"

He's usually so confident that this vulnerability —somehow even more obvious than it was on that first night we spent together— throws me for a loop at first. "Daddy," I bring our foreheads together, "I told you. You're perfect."

London's mouth is on mine before anything more can be said. Dinner is forgotten as our tongues twine together and our hands slip beneath shirts and undo the buttons and flies of our pants. Somewhere along the way, I've swiveled sideways in my seat so we're facing each other properly, and London slips off his chair and sinks to his knees in front of me.

His large hands rest on my thighs, his calloused fingertips toying with the open waistband of my shorts. He looks up at me through thick, dark lashes, the blue of his irises having darkened with his desire. "Can I?"

Lifting my hips in a gesture of silent invitation, I nod.

He doesn't need any further prompting and it's not long before my shorts and underwear are tugged down my legs and thrown aside unceremoniously.

My cock stands at attention for him and I groan when the warmth of his palm wraps around it. London gives it a couple of light pumps before he leans forward and the sweet, wet heat of his mouth envelops the head.

He suckles teasingly, the hand that had gripped me now

trailing light, tickling trails up and down my shaft and over my balls with the tips of his fingers. I want to buck my hips, but I know from experience that he'll only pull off if I do.

London tongues the underside of the crown, putting pressure on my frenulum, driving circles into that sensitive spot with his deliciously devious muscle before licking back up and through the slit.

"*Daddy*," I whine plaintively. "*Please.*"

He takes his wicked time, repeating his actions before slowly taking more of my cock into his mouth until he can't go further. Then he drags back off as torturously slowly, sucking as he goes. These long, languid bobs of his head have me fighting the urge to fuck up into his mouth. My balls draw up and ache with the need to unload, but he's not stimulating me enough to push me over the edge.

I'm a babbling mess of pleas and throbbing desire by the time he finally (*fucking finally*) wraps his hand around the base of my cock and takes pity on me, pumping with firm strokes and hollowing his cheeks. His other hand reaches for my balls, rolling and squeezing them, then moves further back, over the sensitive stretch of skin behind them and then to my needy hole where he slowly rubs his index finger around the rim.

The touch disappears, and I keen desperately, only for him to reach up and place that same finger at my lips. I suck it and his middle finger into my mouth, slicking both up as best I can. He groans around my dick, the vibrations traveling through me with frissons of bliss, then he removes those fingers from my mouth and sends them right back to where I want them the most.

I'm so far gone in the enjoyment of his ministrations that the first finger slips in with very little resistance. The second, lubed only with my spit, burns a bit as he stretches me, but it's a good kind of burn and I shift, spreading my legs wider and leaning back in the chair to give him better access. It's uncomfortable and my back won't thank me for it, but right now I don't care.

I reach out and grip the edge of the dining table when he crooks his fingers and finds my prostate with practiced accuracy.

"London," I breathe. "*Daddy*. I'm so fucking close."

He growls —actually growls— around my cock.

Oh. Right. Language. Whoops.

"S-sorry," I inhale sharply as he twists his tongue and teases the sensitive head of my dick on his next upwards movement. He can spank me later for this final slip of my tongue.

That thought is almost enough to send me over the edge, but I manage to last a few more bobs of his head and curls of his fingers before I unravel, crying out something unintelligible as I spend myself in his mouth.

I don't know what I ever did to deserve this man, this perfect Daddy, but I'll do everything in my power to keep him.

Chapter Twelve — London

"Hayes, you got a minute?" My boss, Stanley, asks, poking his head into my shared office space.

I know there's only one real way to answer that question, so I smother a rueful glance at the half-completed budget estimation for my next project and paste on a solicitous smile. "Sure."

I push back my chair and get to my feet, following him into his office. His is surrounded by the same frosted glass as the boardroom, affording him additional privacy. I close the solid door —painted white like all the others— behind me and take one of the two uncomfortable seats in front of his desk.

Stan steeples his fingers together, seeming to channel Monty Burns as he observes me from the other side of the glass and chrome surface. "You've been kicking goals left and right since you moved into the planner role," he begins, and a part of me relaxes at the compliment.

I'm not being fired. This is a good thing.

"I try," I shrug.

His thin lips quirk upwards. Stan's in his late sixties now and he reminds me a lot of my grandfather. He's short, balding, and stocky. His eyes are a watery sort of blue color, and he's not exactly an imposing figure. Still, he holds all the power here even if he is a pretty good boss, all things considered.

"I've noticed," he tells me after an almost awkward stretch of silence. "Which is why we're lookin' to move you to the new office."

I blink. "What?"

He seems to take my shock as a good sign, even though it's really not. "We're lookin' for someone to manage the team over there. Someone who knows what the company expects of its staff, and who has shown themselves to be a real go-getter. I can't think of anyone better to represent us, London."

This is high praise, especially coming from Stan, but my gut churns with indecision. On the one hand, another promotion so early into my career is kind of amazing. On the other? Taking it means moving to the other side of the country. Away from my friends and my life here.

Away from Matt.

Sure, we've only been together three months at this point, but just the thought of walking away from him makes me feel sick.

"I...I don't know what to say, Stan."

He chortles, missing my blatant reluctance to accept the offer. He'd probably think me insane to turn it down. Part of me knows that it would be crazy if I did. "I know you've only been a planner for a little while, but —let's be honest— you're runnin' rings around Tom, and we know you'll be a good fit for the new site."

"I appreciate that you think so. Really, I do..."

Now my boss's expression begins to fall. He stares back at me, incredulous. "So, what's the problem?"

"You want me to move across the country, right?" He nods. My shoulders slump. "I…" I lick my lips. "My partner is here. I don't think he'll move with me."

There's a flash of surprise on Stan's face, and I realize belatedly that he probably had no idea I was gay. I've always been private about my love life. I don't anticipate any sort of discrimination or anything, but I guess I figured it was easier to remain discreet. Still, even if I was dating a woman, I'd raise the same issue.

Stan leans back in his chair, rubbing his chin and jaw with his palm contemplatively. "I didn't realize you had a relationship to consider, to be honest." He sighs. "That does throw a spanner into the works, doesn't it?"

"Yeah," I exhale. I offer him an apologetic grimace. "I'm sorry. I really would love the job, but…" I trail off.

Once again I remind myself that I've only known Matt for three months. It seems like no time at all in the grand scheme of things. Will I regret turning down this epic career opportunity for something that could end tomorrow?

Guilt washes over me almost immediately at that thought. Matt and I are solid. Yeah, our relationship got serious really quickly, but that's the nature of the lifestyle. And I get far more out of being with him than I ever will from a job. A job I never really planned on having to begin with. I did a psych degree, for fuck's sake!

"Talk to your partner before you turn me down, son." Stan interrupts the whirlpool of thoughts in my head. His tone is understanding and patient. "And I'll see what sort of flexibility we've got up our sleeves here."

Really? Does Stan have that much faith in me that he'd even consider turning the role into something more flexible? Just him saying as much sends a *zing* of pride up my spine.

No, I mightn't have seen myself in this kind of job when I graduated college, but I'm damn good at what I do.

"Okay," I lower my chin, tilting my head appreciatively. "Thank you. I'll talk to him tonight."

Anticipation simmers beneath my skin for the rest of the day.

* * *

"I've got a surprise for you," Matt says by way of greeting when he opens the front door to his place.

He gave me a key last week, but I haven't used it yet. To be honest, while it feels like I've practically moved in, I still don't feel right just waltzing on in. Besides, watching his eyes light up every time he opens the door to find me on the other side makes the idea of using the key less inviting.

We kiss before I say, "And I kinda' have one for you, too."

His brow furrows as he registers my hesitance. "What's wrong?"

"Nothing." That much is certain. I've given it a lot of thought over the course of the day, and no matter what happens with my job, I'm not leaving Matt. "I just need to talk something over with you."

"That sounds fucking ominous."

"Language."

Beneath his beard, his lips quirk. "Sorry, Daddy."

We move into the living room and sit together on the couch. Usually, I'd pull him into my lap or kiss him senseless after a day of separation, but I need to face him right now. I need to see his thoughts play out in his expressions because I know him well enough that he'll try and keep any negative ones from me, still so afraid that I'll walk away if things get too difficult.

"What's going on?" he prods while I consider how to broach the subject.

"So…Stan called me into his office today," I begin, then forge on before he can leap to any incorrect conclusions, "and offered me a pretty big promotion."

The worry which had begun to build in his eyes clears immediately. "That's awesome!"

"Yeah…" Scratching the back of my neck, I watch his face fall again.

"Why aren't you excited about this?"

With a heavy sigh, I admit, "Because they want me to take the Office Manager position at the new location."

"The new…*oh*." Matt knows about the company's expansion because I've mentioned it a couple of times in passing. His face falls and I know where his thoughts are going. I expected as much. Hell, mine would have gone the same way if our roles were reversed.

I reach for his hand, squeezing it. "I'm not leaving, sweetheart."

Confusion contorts his handsome face. "Really?"

"Really."

Now there's guilt in those green eyes of his and it pains me to see it. "But—"

"No. No buts. I've already told my boss I'm not ending my relationship and my life here for a promotion." Running my free hand through my hair, I shrug. "I didn't want to keep this from you, though."

Secrets tend to ruin relationships. I've seen it enough in my life. Secrets, albeit in regard to infidelity, destroyed my parents' marriage. Having watched them fail spectacularly at communicating, I've never wanted to repeat those mistakes. So far, I think Matt and I have done well not to fall into that trap. Now's not the time to start.

"*London…*" Matt shakes his head in disbelief. He sounds awed and horrified all at once. "This is too good an opportunity for you. You work so hard. You shouldn't let it go."

"I'm not taking the job if it means having to let you go," I reiterate, warmed by the relief that flickers over his face. "Stan said that they'd look into how flexible they could be. Maybe that means fly-in fly-out or working remotely or something. But if they can't, I'm still choosing you, sweetheart." I can't help grinning at him now, because this is the part that I've been focused on all day. The pinnacle that everything has boiled down to. "I love you, Matt."

A myriad of emotions swim in his eyes at my declaration, but he doesn't leave me hanging. A huge smile tugs his lips upwards, and he brings our foreheads together. "I love you, too."

We're kissing before anything more can be said. Even though these feelings have been building for months, putting the words out there seems to add even more intensity to the meeting of our lips. We kiss slowly and deeply, as though rediscovering each other. I pull Matt into my lap, guiding his strong thighs to straddle mine, gripping and squeezing his ass over his jeans as I grind up against him with our mouths fused together. Beard burn be damned, I never want this kiss to end.

Most evenings when I come over after work, I help Matt get into his Little mind space and we're content to spend the most of our time together as Daddy and boy. But today I'm glad he's big. I'm glad we've been able to talk and exchange mutual declarations of our feelings.

Don't get me wrong: I enjoy being his Daddy, and I don't mind if he's little more often than not (even if having sex with him in Littlespace was something I did first reach out to talk to Charlie about because it turned out *that* was where I became a bit conflicted with the lifestyle) but I'm pleased we were on equal footing when I told him that I loved him for the first time.

"Oh," Matt's almost surprised murmur pulls me from my thoughts at the same time he disengages from the kiss, "I almost forgot *my* surprise for *you*."

With my cock aching between too many layers of fabric, I'm half tempted to tell him it can wait. But then I look into his eyes which are practically dancing with excitement, and I can't deny him. Especially not when it's something he's arranged for me.

Still, I do complain as he climbs off my lap and tugs me to my feet, ushering me into the master bedroom. "I do like bedroom surprises," I joke with a laugh as he enthusiastically drags me along by the hand.

"Well, this is kind of for me as much as it is for you," Matt says, suddenly sounding a little uncertain before he steps aside and I finally see the bed. Or, rather, the carefully laid out lingerie on top of the bed.

An array of satin and lace has been carefully arranged over the navy bedspread in a veritable rainbow of colors. There are panties and thongs, a couple of camisoles, a sheer black negligee and even a stunning corset. As I step in for a closer look, I can tell that he's picked out quality items, many of which

I've had sitting in my online wish list, that I know have cost him a small fortune.

"*Matt…*" I breathe, not knowing what to say. "This is…" Beautiful. Amazing. Too much. Perfect. "*Wow.*"

"You like them?" His voice is smaller again. Uncertain. He's not Little Matty right now, but he's not used to taking charge or making grand gestures like this (that's more my role) and my stunned silence is probably doing more harm than good in this situation.

"Sweetheart, I love them," I reach out to finger the sheer negligee, the material softer and smoother under my fingertips than I anticipated. I want nothing more than to strip off my business attire and slip it on instead. Somehow, I refrain. Turning to Matt, I ask in wonderment, "But…why?"

The vulnerability and insecurity melts away from his expression. "I just wanted to do something nice for you," he explains with a shrug. "And, like I said, seeing you wearing them is a gift to myself, really." He reaches across in front of me and picks up a lacy red camisole and matching thong. "This is my favorite of the lot. I think it'll look hot as fu…er…*sin* on you."

"Good boy," I praise his self-censoring, then reach for the items he's holding. "Then I guess I shouldn't keep you waiting, huh? Better make sure they fit at the very least."

Matt nods enthusiastically and practically shoves the set into my hands, pushing me towards the bathroom to change. Through the partially closed door that separates us, I can hear him hurriedly removing the rest of the lingerie from the bed, and he loudly declares that he's putting it all away in my underwear drawer (the one he cleared out for me a couple of months earlier) for me to sort through later.

I toss the clothes I had been wearing into the hamper before

I carefully pull on the scrap of thin material masquerading as a thong, adjusting my balls and still hard cock inside the lace. I don't glance into the mirror above the sink until I've also slipped the camisole over my head.

I've never gone beyond just panties and thongs, so the silky, thin material across my pecs and spaghetti straps over my shoulders feel foreign to me. I'm concerned that my reflection will appear ridiculous, but after fiddling with the straps so that the cami hangs comfortably, I finally look at myself.

Whoa.

Matt was right. The bright red pops against my pale skin and black hair, and it seems to make my eyes bluer. I still look like a stocky man wearing delicate, effeminate clothing, but I can't say that it looks *bad*. Just…different.

Lifting the hem of my camisole, I turn to the side, admiring my tight ass cheek and the sliver of red material peeking out from my crack and stretching over my hip. Facing forward again, I can see the tip of my cock peeking out from the top band of the front of the thong, glistening with precum. I drop the thin, almost see-through material and the hem reaches to just above the tops of my thighs, the material fluttering against the tip of my cock as I move.

"*Daddy,*" the plaintive whine from the bedroom jerks me from my thoughts. "Are you dressed yet? I'm dying here."

I can't help but chuckle. We were both worked up before I stepped away to try on some of his gifts, and 'patient' isn't exactly a word I'd use to describe my boy at the best of times.

"Coming, sweetheart," I call back.

"That's the plan!"

I want to spank him for the sass, but I'm too horny and too excited to see his reaction to me wearing the lingerie he picked out to act on that urge. Instead, I take one last look in the mirror and stride to the door, swinging it open and striding into the bedroom with purpose.

Matt's already on the bed, naked, lying on his side with his head propped on his hand, his other hand palming his leaking cock. When he sees me, his jaw goes slack. "Holy shit," he growls out, his voice low and needy.

"Language."

"Sorry, but have you seen yourself?" He spreads precum over the head of his cock and then down the shaft, squeezing himself on his next upstroke. His eyes are practically blazing with desire. "That was justified cussing."

"Oh, was it now?" I stalk forward, my amusement warring with my need to replace his hand with mine. Or with my mouth. Or to roll him onto his back and pound into him with abandon. Or…well, anything that would lead to the intense orgasms I know we're going to share soon. "Pretty sure it's still breaking the rules, baby."

Matt remains unrepentant, those green eyes of his traveling over my body shamelessly. "I think I should get a pass this time," he argues, cocking an eyebrow at me when he finally looks up at my face again. "Because you love me…and I bought you all those pretty things."

The uncharacteristic mischief in his voice and his playfully bratty behavior tells me he's been spending time with Josh. I don't envy the Daddy who gets to take that boy in hand, even if I do consider Josh a friend these days.

Still, I'm not letting Matt push the boundaries too far, even if I do want to laugh and pin him to the mattress.

"*Matteo*," I warn, smirking when he groans and closes his eyes.

"Sorry, Daddy."

"Good boy."

Another moan escapes him. *"London,"* he pleads, "you're killing me."

Taking pity on him —or, really, on myself, because I can't remember the last time I was this hard— I close the distance between us and roll him onto his back so I can crawl over him, allowing his hands to roam over the camisole he bought for me. He obediently spreads his legs and I grind my cock against his, the soft lace between us becoming wet with the evidence of our mutual arousal.

"I love the lingerie, sweetheart," I whisper against his lips, my breath teasing him, knowing that he wants me to close that last little bit of distance and kiss him stupid.

"Me too," he agrees, teasing my nipples through the silky soft fabric that covers them. "It's like wrapping paper for the world's best present."

This time, I can't contain my chuckles. "God, I love you." It's a thrill to say those words again, this time pressed against him in bed as we are, practically naked and writhing.

This seems to push him beyond the limits of his control and he surges forward, capturing my lips and rolling us until we've switched positions. Then his hands pull down the thong I'm wearing, throwing it across the room, and he straddles my hips.

"Whoa," I wrench our lips apart when he guides the tip of my cock to his hole. "Stop. Lube, babe."

Sitting up, still straddling me, Matt smirks down at me and gestures to the open bottle of lube on the bedside table. "You were taking your time getting changed," he explains, "so...I took a little initiative."

He prepped for me. I smother a groan. "Next time, I want to

watch," I tell him, hearing the gravelly quality of my own voice while my dick jerks at the images my brain has conjured. "But, fuck, sweetheart, if that's not the hottest thing ever..."

Still, my fingers travel beneath him, wanting to be sure that he's ready to go. I sink two in with very little resistance and scissor them while he works his hips.

"*Please...*" Matt practically whimpers when I deliberately graze his prostate.

"Okay, baby. Okay." I grab for the lube and slick my cock up, clicking the cap shut and tossing the bottle back in the general direction of Matt's side of the bed. "Ride me, sweetheart."

He doesn't need to be told twice. We both moan as he slowly sinks down on top of me until I've bottomed out. I give him a moment to breathe and adjust, and then he begins to move, bouncing on my cock in earnest.

I love watching him like this. His golden skin glistens with a thin sheen of sweat, and his muscles ripple with every movement. But the best part is watching him control his own pleasure. He sets the pace, clenching around my cock on every upward motion, swiveling his hips and taking what he needs from me while I rock my own hips up to meet him at the rhythm he's setting.

When my hand closes around his cock, pumping him in time with his bouncing, he throws his head back, his mouth falling open as his eyes drift shut. His hands drift over my camisole, though, traveling the peaks and valleys of my skin over the now sweat-dampened fabric.

I can tell he's getting close, knowing the signs of his impending orgasm as well as I know my own now. His breathing hitches and his fingers clench in the lace over my pecs while he picks up speed with his hips.

"Da…Daddy," he pants, "London…fu…uuuhhh," I want to chuckle at the way he only just manages to censor himself, but I'm about to go over the edge myself. "Coming. I'm…*ungh*… I'm *coming*."

I love the way he makes the declaration, despite the fact that it's not something I can miss happening. I don't even think he knows he's doing it. He's just vocal and it's all sorts of hot and endearing all at once.

I shout incoherently as his orgasm pulls mine from me, the clenching around my cock milking everything I've got. He slumps down on top of me, my cock still inside him, while we catch our breaths. We're a sweaty, sticky, sated mess and I'm awash in the afterglow of our exuberant love making.

It just reaffirms my decision to choose my relationship over my potential promotion. Work could never make me feel this content.

"I love you," Matt says, nuzzling his bearded face into the crook of my neck. "You said it again and I didn't."

Snickering, I rub my hand soothingly over his back. "We're not keeping score, baby. But I do like hearing you say it."

"Mmm," he nibbles at my skin, almost as if he can't get enough of me. "Then I'll say it every chance I get."

"Me too, sweetheart. I promise."

Chapter Thirteen — Matteo

I should feel guilty that London turned down a promotion for me. I really should. But, instead, all I can feel is relief. It's a strange sensation to be someone's priority, but an addictive one all the same. That said, we talked about it some more over dinner last night, and I made it clear that if his company is willing to be flexible, London should still consider his options.

I'd love to be able to make some sort of grand gesture of my own, to offer to move with him and uproot my own life, but that's not really feasible. I've only just settled in here. I have close friends for the first time in over a decade. I have a job I enjoy, and I love living in the home I grew up in. I felt insanely selfish for telling him these things, but London just shook his head and gave me one of his indulgent smiles and reassured me that he understood.

I've really lucked out with him.

I float through my workday, riding on the endorphins from last night. Between finally saying those three little words to each other, hearing London tell me that he'll choose me over his job and then seeing him rock the sexy as hell lingerie I bought for him, I honestly feel like maybe I'm dreaming. If I am, though, I don't want to wake up.

When Ash calls me after I finish work, we agree to meet for beers at a little hole in the wall bar that's roughly halfway between our houses. It's a relaxed space, with scuffed cement floors and a hipster-industrial atmosphere. I get there before Ash and find a tall table with high, wrought-iron bar stools, snagging it for us and ordering two of the daily special brews, seeing as the drinks menu here rotates frequently.

Jesse, the guy behind the bar, grins at me as he hands over two tall glasses of pale ale, his dirty-blonde man-bun wobbling on top of his head as he excitedly tells me all about the brew I'm about to try. I'm not all that interested in hearing about the hops or the fruity infusion or whatever, but his passion for supporting local micro-breweries is actually kind of sweet, so I nod and make appropriate sounds of appreciation as required.

I'm still relieved when Ash saunters through the door and waves at me.

"That's my cue," I tell Jesse with feigned regret, lifting the beers in a gesture of thanks before sliding back over to the table I commandeered earlier. "Thanks."

He waves me off and I set the glasses down on the worn timber table top before greeting Ash with a quick hug. He slips his messenger bag from his shoulder and drops it on top of the table next to his beer with a grateful sigh.

"Long day?" I ask.

He's gone back to only working part time at Ted's firm so that he can work on finishing his college degree. I know he hates studying, but with only two semesters to go at part-time (or one at full-time), Ash decided it made no sense not to see it out to the end. Besides, once he realized that he could put the knowledge and skills to work with Charlie's business plans, that has only made him more determined to graduate.

"My statistics professor can kiss my ass," he complains, dropping onto the stool across the table from me with a huff. "The assignment he's set is worth fifty percent of my grade and it's brutal."

"Do you need help?" It's no secret that I'm good with numbers, data and extrapolation. "I can look over your work before you submit it if you want."

Ash's smile turns grateful. "I'd love that. All my other classes are fine, but stats aren't my thing."

We chat about the parameters of his assignment for a while and I offer him some pointers before he drains his glass and hisses through his teeth. "Okay, no more college talk. My brain is fried. I can't handle it."

I chuckle and nod, finishing the last of my drink as well. "That's fair, dude. Take a break; it sounds like you've earned it."

"Amen to that." He swings around on his stool, slinking off it with the grace of youth and his slimmer frame. Snagging our glasses, he tells me the next round is on him and he crosses the narrow walkway between our table and the bar before I can argue.

I watch him banter with Jesse for a minute before he returns with two new glasses brimming with golden liquid and the perfect froth ratio. I thank him as I take my first drag from the new glass. The liquid is crisp and refreshing, even though I've already polished off one glass already.

"Okay, so I've whined enough about my day," Ash settles himself back on his seat, running his finger through the condensation on the side of his glass while he cocks his head at me. "Your turn. How's your week going?"

I can't suppress the wide, happy smile that splits my face as I remember yesterday all over again.

"Well," my best friend's expression brightens to match mine, "that good, huh?" He leans across the table and places his hand over my forearm. "I'm glad to see it, Matt. Really. London's perfect for you."

"He is," I agree. "We, uh, we did the whole 'I love you' thing yesterday." I can feel my cheeks turning pink. "This whole thing has felt kind of surreal, but…" I trail off, shaking my head, unable to really put my jumbled mess of feelings and thoughts into words.

"Hey, I get it," Ash laughs. "Remember, it wasn't that long ago I was in the same boat. Well, maybe a similar boat." He takes another sip of his drink then licks his lips contemplatively. He's a couple of years younger than London, but has the same mature outlook on life. I know that, in his case, it's because he had a rough upbringing with his asshole dad…and that makes me wonder whether London's the same.

London and I have obviously spoken about our pasts and our personal baggage some, but he hasn't really gone into detail about his childhood. I know he's the child of a messy divorce, and that he adores his mother beyond words, but, to be honest, he doesn't mention his dad very often. There's a tiny part of me that worries he's into me (or older men in general) because he's got Daddy issues. Which, okay, given our kinky relationship and the roles we play, is really kind of hilarious.

"…fast, right?"

I shake my head, offering my friend a sheepish smile. "Sorry," I apologize. "I got lost in thought for a minute there." I lift my glass and eye him over the rim. "You were saying?"

Asher's smile is understanding, as though he can guess where my thoughts went. He wouldn't be completely wrong, even if he thought I was thinking naughtier thoughts about my man than I actually was.

"I was just saying that it feels like things are going fast, right? Like...things got serious kinda' quickly?" Ash shrugs and sets down his beer, staring into it with a more serious expression on his face while he continues to muse aloud. "Things *really* flew with Charlie. In hindsight, it was almost scary how we went from complete strangers to falling for each other within weeks. Maybe even days. But," he looks back up at me, a secretive grin toying with the corners of his lips, "I've read, and the guys have all agreed, that it's not wholly unexpected in the lifestyle, y'know? I mean, Charlie and I did go a lot faster than most, I think, but I...I needed that. I needed to feel wanted and grounded and looked after."

"I can relate to that," I nod. "And as long as you were both comfortable with it, who cares how fast you guys went? I mean, I gave London a key a month ago, when we'd only been together for two months."

I know that Ash moved in with Charlie the day they met, but those were extenuating circumstances.

He bobs his head. "Like I said, I think a lot of it comes down to the lifestyle. As Littles, we put a lot of trust in these guys and get attached to them in ways more traditional or vanilla relationships take additional time to develop or whatever."

I can see his point. It's not even the careful balance of power between the Daddy and boy roles, either. At least, not to me. Giving him control isn't about being bossed around, but about letting him handle all the things that stress me out. There's something about the amount of emotion that builds when Daddy's being so nurturing. Something about letting go and being insanely vulnerable, and knowing that Daddy not only cares about my Little side, but genuinely enjoys being my caregiver as much as I love having someone look after me like he does.

But with London there's the additional level of trust he puts in me. I know that he has his hang ups about being a big, strong man who gets off on wearing frilly, lacy underwear, but he still lets me see him as he explores his kink. The feeling I get knowing that I'm the only person to ever see him do so is intoxicating.

There's a real give and take between us, and that's definitely helped to shuttle us along in our relationship.

"You're right," I tell Ash in response to his musings. "And I'm okay with that. We're still taking things step-by-step, even if the steps are coming on quickly."

Ash clinks our glasses together, his shiny engagement ring glinting with the movement. He winks. "I'll drink to that."

* * *

"Daddy?" I squirm when London looks at me from over the top of his book.

It's finally Saturday and we're chilling at home; he's reading while I play with my blocks on the mat in front of the couch. His bosses are still discussing just how flexible they can be with the position they've offered him, so we haven't had to revisit the discussion about his job and what those changes might mean for us. Still, it's lurking in the back of my brain constantly and, even though I know he loves me, I've started to let doubts creep in about his choices. Because he can read me as well as the fantasy novels he enjoys so much, London insisted I let go and get some additional Little time in to try and settle my anxieties.

"What's up, sweetheart?"

I bite my lip, second-guessing the urge that overtook me enough to interrupt his reading. We've talked about this before, but I've never worked up the courage to ask for it. Something about our exchange earlier in the week, knowing that he loves me, pushed me enough to get his attention, though. And with how deeply little I want to get around him, if I can get the words out, I think it'll help me.

"Matt?" Daddy prompts, sliding his bookmark in between the pages of his novel and setting the book aside so he can give me his full attention.

I wriggle in place, wondering why it's so difficult to ask for what I want. I remind myself that he'll safe word if he's at all uncomfortable. He loves me. He trusts me. And I trust him. Still, I avert my gaze as I ask, "*Can-you-help-me-go-potty?*" all in one breath.

I can hear the sounds of his clothes rustling and the soft footsteps he takes before his bare feet enter my field of vision. Then he crouches down in front of me, tilting my chin up so I have to look him in the eye. He smiles at me and kisses me on the forehead. "I'm proud of you for asking, baby." Then he stands and offers me his hand. I take it and he helps me to my feet.

"Traffic light?" I ask him, searching those blue eyes for even a hint of discomfort or disgust.

"Green." He replies without hesitation. "You?"

I love that he still asks me, even though I'm the one who

suggested trying this new thing. "Green."

Guiding me to the bathroom, he leads me to the toilet and helps me pull down the play shorts and training pants he dressed me in earlier. Then he steps in close behind me, pressing his chest against my back, and holds his hand over mine while he helps me aim over the bowl as I pee.

"Good boy," he praises after giving me a couple of quick shakes, reaching for a couple of squares of toilet paper to give me a brief dab before tucking my cock back into my training pants, resettling my shorts around my hips.

We wash and dry our hands and, after he leads me back into the living room, he tugs me into his lap.

The entire experience was over within a couple of minutes at most, and I'm bewildered to feel like it was *normal*. A complete non-event.

I mean, yeah, having someone else's hands on me while I peed did feel a bit strange, but I was expecting to feel more embarrassment or *something*. Instead, it just felt exactly like what it was: Daddy helping his boy. Nothing beyond that. Hell, the diapering process is more intimate and confronting than this was.

"You okay, baby?" Daddy asks, nuzzling the back of my neck with his nose.

I snort. "I guess I expected that to feel weirder than it did." I turn, trying to meet his gaze. "Was it weird for you at all?"

"Nope." Again, there's no hesitation in his response. "Did you want it to feel differently?"

I consider the question before I shake my head in the negative. "No. Not really." I scrunch my nose. "I thought it would be something bigger, y'know? But it was…nice? That's not the right word. It…" I huff out a breath, frustrated that I can't quite express what I'm feeling. "I think it'll help me stay little next time. I mean... if you're comfortable with it."

His lips find my temple. "I am," he assures me, his voice rumbling up his chest. "And if you decide to take it further...if you want to use your diapers...I'm okay with that, too."

Huh.

"Is that something *you're* curious about?"

London pauses for a moment, but I don't sense any indecision. If anything, the silence is thoughtful. "I suppose I am," he answers after a few seconds. "I just feel like it's a pretty big part of the lifestyle; one I haven't experienced." He shrugs. "It's nothing we have to rush into, but it seems like the next step from what we just did, right?" Then he chuckles. "Or, I guess, if you think about it in terms of natural progression in childhood development, we skipped the step entirely."

I snort at that. "The age regression thing is *technically* going backwards, right? So, by that logic, it's reverse development and it would be the next step."

"Reverse development," he repeats with another laugh and a shake of his head. "That's not a thing."

"Well, I'm making it a thing."

His thick, stocky fingers tickle my sides. I'm not all that ticklish, but he knows exactly which spot to hit in order to make me flinch away with as manly a squeal as I can muster.

I love these moments with him. I can't actually recall ever being this silly or carefree with Trent, which almost makes me sad because I spent ten years with him. Ten years without this kind of freedom and joy. I can't say I regret the relationship because, without it, I doubt I would have made the choices that eventually brought me to this moment, but I do mourn for the man I might have been under different circumstances.

147

"Hey," London's hand is smoothing up and down my back. "Where'd you just go, sweetheart?"

I shake off the melancholy my hypothetical musings have induced and lean back against my lover's chest. "I was just thinking about how lucky I am to have you as my Daddy."

"We're both lucky," he insists, cuddling me closer. "And it doesn't matter which steps we take, or when. We're in this together for the long haul, okay?"

I nod, feeling suddenly, unexpectedly choked up. "Yes, Daddy."

God, I love this man.

Chapter Fourteen — London

We don't revisit the diaper conversation again. At least, not over the course of the next week. Instead, Stan sits me down on Wednesday to tell me that he and his business partners have gone over their options, which gives me something else to focus on.

"If you're willing to spend every second week at the new site for the next six months, the job's yours," he says with a toothy grin. "If all goes as well as I think it will, and you train your people up to be nice and autonomous, we can look at minimizing the schedule after that and have you working remotely from here with maybe a monthly visit to the new site from there on out."

Stan's leaning back in his cushy, high-backed leather office chair, his fingers interlaced behind his head. He looks like the cat who caught the damn canary.

My heart thumps in my chest. It's a better compromise than I had anticipated they'd come up with, but I'll still be away from Matt for entire weeks at a time.

But I'll also be here for entire weeks, too.

The fact that the company is willing to spend money on return airfares every other week is mind boggling. But...where would I stay? If I let up the lease on my apartment, I could probably afford to stay in a motel or something every other week. Something low budget. I'd only need a place to sleep and shower, really. But, if I did that, would Matt mind me moving into his place on the weeks when I'm here? I know I've basically moved in as it is, but even I know that I'm being presumptuous to think I could just spend every other week living in his house without discussing this all first.

"Can I discuss this with Matt, first?" I ask my boss. "My partner, I mean." We haven't really spoken about the potential promotion since I first brought it up. With the idea of flexibility in limbo, there was nothing to really talk about. But now there is, and I won't make this decision without his input. "I told him that you were looking into options, but we didn't really want to guess what that might mean."

Stan smiles indulgently because he can tell that I'm interested in the offer. As far as he's concerned, my talking it over with Matt is a formality at best, I'm sure. But if Matt isn't on board, I'm still turning Stan down.

* * *

"I think you have to take the job," Matt tells me over dinner. I've explained Stan's offer and, even though I tried to remain neutral, I'm pretty sure he can see straight through me. He doesn't seem upset or worried, though, and that goes a long way to settling my anxieties about accepting the promotion.

"Yeah?" I ask, wanting to be absolutely certain this won't

hurt us as a couple. "You'd be okay with that? Even though it means me being gone half the time?"

With his grilled chicken breast half-eaten, Matt carefully puts his cutlery down on the table and looks me in the eye. "It's for six months, and it's better than the alternative where you could have taken the original job offer and moved across the country permanently." When I move to say something —to argue, or to reassure him, or some mixture of both— he holds up a hand to stop me. "But, more than that, we're solid. We can Facetime or whatever while you're over there, and we'll just have to make up for lost time when you're back home."

Home.

The word warms me from the inside. "We can do that," I nod, waggling my eyebrows at him suggestively.

Matt shakes his head with a soft smile. He reaches for my hand across the timber tabletop and squeezes it. "Move in with me. Make this your home for real."

Even though I'd had the same thought earlier today, it blows my mind to hear him asking me. He hasn't had to make many big decisions (or even smaller ones) since we met, since I became his Daddy...and this is *huge*.

"Are you sure?" I ask him, my eyes not leaving his. "I won't lie; I want that more than anything right now. But I don't want you to feel pressured here."

If I squint, I can see parallels to my parents' relationship and I'm still terrified of repeating my dad's mistakes.

Matt needs to know what he's getting himself into. Even though I know I'm not my father, that my situation with Matt is different to the resentful aspiring artist who knocked his girlfriend up, I still share that guy's genetic makeup.

Holding up a hand before Matt can dive all the way in, I

confess, "I really need you to be sure, baby. Because I don't want either of us becoming resentful or bitter or—"

"Hey," usually it's me calming him, but right now the tables are turned. As if our roles really are reversed, Matt looks every bit his age when he gently cups my cheek and asks, "where'd that come from?"

Then I tell him everything. Obviously, he knew the basics of my baggage before now, but now I fill in the blanks. My parents were young —in their early twenties— and had a whirlwind romance which resulted in me. My dad felt pressured to stick around. To move my mother in. To play happy families when all he'd wanted to do was see the world as a free spirit. He took a job which involved a lot of traveling, and ultimately a lot of infidelity. Then, after mom found out and they had a huge fight, he walked out completely, leaving her heartbroken.

"I don't want to repeat his mistakes," I explain, sounding miserable and young to my own ears. "And I know it's not the same thing, but we've gone fast and..." I lift my palms up in a gesture that's stuck somewhere between begging and shrugging, "what if I'm like him after all?"

Matt listens through the entire confession, and it strikes me that we really have come full-circle. Only when we started this whole thing, he was the one needing the catharsis of an emotional purge. Now it's me.

"Well," Matt muses aloud, a soft, understanding smile playing on his lips, "that answers a lot of questions for me."

I feel crestfallen at those words. I've tried so hard to be open, to communicate properly, but if he still had questions...

"Stop it," Matt's firm voice interrupts my spiraling thoughts. He reaches out to hold my face between his large, warm palms and stares me in the eye. It's so rare that he takes charge, that his expression or tone match his physical appearance, that I sit in stunned silence while he says, "We're both far more mature than that, London. And, yeah, I might prefer to sink into Littlespace and let you call the shots, but if I had any doubts at all, I'd tell you. Just like I trust that you would tell me. I mean, you just did." He leans in and kisses me. "The fact that you're trying not to repeat your parents' mistakes proves that you probably won't. I can't know the future, but I don't think we're at risk that way. So," he smiles again, "move in with me."

"You're sure?" I sound like a broken record. "It's really not too fast for you?"

It's only been three months. I love him, but I won't forgive myself for rushing him.

"I would have moved you in that first night if it wouldn't have made me seem like a clingy, crazy person," he assures me with a self-deprecating chuckle. "I'm nuts about you, London. I get that this feels like we're moving fast, but, at my age, I'm at the point where I can't let the best things in my life slip through my fingers just because I've assigned some sort of arbitrary number to how long I think society expects I should wait to have them."

Well, then. I can't argue with that, can I? Not when I feel the same way. Even if I am practically half his age, I know better than to overthink my instincts. I love him, he loves me, and we both want this.

A smile stretches across my face. "When can I move in?"

* * *

"Are you sure you want to donate all of this?" Charlie asks me on the following Saturday, standing in the middle of the living room in my apartment. He gestures at my barely used Ikea furniture. The sectional couch is as pristine as the day I bought it, and the coffee table also looks new.

"I'm keeping the bookshelves," I remind him, "but Matt's place is fully furnished, so I don't have any use for any of it."

Matt steals a kiss as he saunters past, lugging a huge box of books as though he's carrying a pile of pillows. Those muscles of his aren't just for decoration after all. "Are you sure you aren't attached to anything? What about your bed?" he asks me. "Because we can replace the one in the spare room with yours if you want."

"Nah," I wave the suggestion away. "I don't have any sentimental attachments to my furniture. I'd rather it go to someone in need." Which is why I've told Charlie to take it all and do with it what he will. Apparently, he's organized a storage unit for most of it, with plans to use it in his safe house/community center project as I'd hoped.

I bend down and heft up my own box of books, groaning under its weight. "As long as I've got my books and my clothes, I'm good."

It wasn't until Matt and I started to pack up my things that I realized just how minimalist my life has been until now. I don't have much in the way of knickknacks or personal effects. A fuckton of books, yeah, and a wardrobe full of clothes, but not much else. My kitchen cupboards contain the bare minimum in terms of cutlery and cookware, and all of my childhood photo albums are still at my mom's house a couple hours' drive away. So all I'm moving across to Matt's place are books, clothing, my big TV, neglected PS4 and a handful of games Matt doesn't already own.

I follow Matt to the car and load the boxes into the backseat, the trunk of my Hyundai stuffed to the brim with my clothes. The trunk of his car is packed with boxes, too. Cutting my lease short proved to be relatively easy, and all the guys volunteered to help empty out my place the second Matt mentioned it in the group chat.

"Last chance to back out," I tease my lover, crossing my wrists behind his neck to draw him in for another kiss. It feels like I'm trying to stockpile them, knowing that spending every second week apart is going to be painful until we're used to the routine.

Matt rubs our noses together. "Not a chance, Daddy."

I dive in for another kiss, this one less innocent.

"Oh, I see how it is," Chance's voice interrupts us, and Matt sighs into my mouth before he pulls back to glare at his friend, who drops another box at our feet, unrepentant. "You've got us all doing the heavy lifting while you guys dry hump out here."

"Crude," Matt accuses the somewhat scruffy ginger-haired man.

"Says the guy playing tonsil hockey with his toyboy." Chance taunts back with a wink to let us know he's only playing.

I roll my eyes, taking the bait as is expected of me. "He's the Boy and you know it, bud." I cock my head. "Speaking of Boys, you've been very quiet in the chat lately, Chance. Any news you'd like to share with the group?"

Matt perks up at that, picking up the needling where I've left off. "Are you holding out on us? Is there a new Little in your life?"

"Fuck you both," Chance laughs, shaking his head. He gestures between us. "Go back to mauling each other already."

"That's not a denial," Matt observes, grinning knowingly.

Chance rolls his eyes. "If you must know, I've been on a few dates and tried a few scenes with a guy, but we're probably not going anywhere." He shrugs when he catches the matching grimaces of commiseration on our faces. "It was worth giving it a shot, but neither one of us is devastated that it hasn't worked out."

"Still, I'm sorry," Matt apologizes, guilt painting his expression. "I shouldn't have pushed the subject." I give him a squeeze, proud of how empathetic he is.

"Nah," Chance waves him off. "No harm, no foul. Serves me right for not mentioning it in the chat. It's not a big thing."

"Still…" I begin to object, but my words are cut off as Josh interrupts our impromptu pow-wow.

"What are you all standing around here for?" He asks, hefting one end of my tall, oak bookshelf. Spencer's got the other end and they're carrying it towards his truck, which is parked on the street just past the driveway to my apartment complex. Despite his leaner, more wiry frame, Spencer doesn't appear to be struggling under the weight of the timber like I might have expected. He's obviously stronger than he looks.

"Chance was just telling us to stop slacking off," I answer smoothly, and Matt hugs me tighter to his side, clearly appreciating my choice to keep Chance's woes among ourselves.

Oblivious, Josh grins at the bearded ginger man. "You caught them making out like teenagers, right? They've been doing it all day."

"We have not," Matt argues back with a childish lilt.

Letting out a bark of laughter, I tilt my head from side to side and smile at him. "I mean…we kinda' have, sweetheart." If I had to make an educated guess, I'd say that the anticipation and joy of officially moving in together has gotten to us both.

He takes his hand in mine and his expression turns almost goofy. "I can't help it," he declares after a few moments, "you're moving in." His words echo my thoughts as though we're in sync with each other. "I'm…well, I'm excited, I guess."

"Me too, baby." Assuring him comes as natural to me as breathing. I lean in so that my lips brush his earlobe as I whisper, "And I'll show you how much just as soon as I can get you alone and naked."

"Mmm," he murmurs back, turning his head so that his beard rubs my cheek, "do we have to get completely naked? Because I don't think I have the patience for that."

"Ugh," Josh complains good-naturedly, shooting me a wink before he starts backing towards Spencer's truck, practically dragging the other man along, "get a room."

"We're working on it," Matt sasses back.

"Yeah," Spencer finally chimes in, shifting the weight of the bookshelf in his grip, "it might even go a bit faster if you actually *worked* right now."

Stealing one last kiss in the form of a quick peck of the lips, I chuckle and take a step back from Matt with my hands held in surrender. "Alright, point taken," I acknowledge, feeling only a little guilty that these guys have been doing the bulk of the heavy lifting for the past few minutes. "I'll even throw in an extra case of beer tonight as a peace offering."

"Add extra pizza and all is forgiven," Chance throws over his shoulder on his way back into my apartment building.

I follow him and clap him on the shoulder. "You drive a hard bargain."

As a group, we continue to banter while we disassemble the apartment and take it down to the trucks outside. It takes a couple of hours, but it would have taken longer without Matt's friends, who I have also come to see as my own friends.

It strikes me, as we're all sprawled out through the living

room in Matt's house (*our* house now), that I really had been living a pretty lonely existence before Matt.

Sure, I'd been busy, and I'd had surface friendships with guys from college and people I worked with, but outside of Cherie and Kate, I hadn't really connected properly with anyone. I could psychoanalyze myself for years if I wanted to, but I know that I'd been holding myself back. Until Matt.

Meeting Matt forced me to acknowledge a side of myself I'd pushed aside. He might say that he's the needy one in our relationship, but, as far as I'm concerned, that goes both ways. I think I needed someone to take care of just as badly as he needed someone to care for him. And, once I opened myself up to him, connecting with other people came easier.

"What're you thinking about?" Matt asks, nudging me with his shoulder.

Later, I'll divulge all of my revelations, but right now I just kiss him on the cheek and nuzzle his neck. "Just thinking how lucky I am to have found you, sweetheart."

"We're both lucky, Daddy."

Well, I can't argue with that.

So I don't.

Chapter Fifteen — Matteo

The first three months of London's fly-in, fly-out routine sucked hard. It took us a while to not only get used to not seeing each other every second week, but to also manage the time difference between us. I struggled badly enough during the first month that I earned myself my first genuine disciplinary spanking on London's second week back in town, because a week without my Daddy and without any intervening Little time had manifested in some bratty tantrums I'm not proud of.

But, after some trial and error, we were able to make it work.

On the weeks London's been across the country, I've had Little time at Ash and Charlie's place, much like I did prior to meeting my Daddy. It's not the same, but it's enough to take the edge off, and I know that Ash loves having me around for playdates. Josh even joins us occasionally, and some of the other guys are also happy to step in as caregivers when Charlie's got meetings.

On the weeks where London *is* in town, I try not to monopolize his personal time too much. We live together, so I get him all night every night, and that makes it easier to share him with Cherie and Kate, or even the guys when they drop in to hang out. I'm usually little during these catch ups, wanting to maximize my alone time with London when I'm big.

Now that we're midway through the fifth month of London's trial of his new role, things feel pretty settled. It's a Friday night and the whole gang is over at our place. We're at the tail end of a belated birthday get-together for London, who turned twenty-seven last week. We celebrated in private with some mutual masturbation via Facetime on the day, and when he flew back in I gave him his gifts (some new lingerie and a spectacular blowjob) the first night he was home. But tonight, the group convened for dinner, drinks, and playtime.

Right now, Ash, Katie and I are all little, but so is Josh, which is a surprise. More often than not, even on my playdates at Ash's place, he remains big.

I wonder if work has been stressful for him because I've never seen him sink so readily into Littlespace. Even Charlie's keeping a cautious eye on him, which is telling. But, in Littlespace, Josh is boisterous and happy, so I'm not too worried. I understand how freeing this aspect of the lifestyle can be and, as a cop, he probably deserves to be released from grown-up worries more than most of us.

When I get up from my spot on the rug playing with the new Duplo set Daddy bought me recently, Daddy shoots me a questioning glance. He's been sitting on the end of the couch next to Charlie, nursing a bottle of beer and chatting about adult stuff that, honestly, I'm more than happy to tune out when I'm little. But, even though he's engaged in that conversation, his focus never really leaves me. As always, I can't help but enjoy that sign that he genuinely cares about me.

"Just gotta pee," I tell him as I move to pass him and head towards the master suite.

His hand reaches out, grabbing mine to stop my movement, and he tugs me down to murmur in my ear, "You're diapered, babe."

I blink at him, surprised that he's bringing it up, that we're having *that* implied conversation now with all our friends around us. But his voice is pitched low, his words murmured for my privacy. Not that I really need it: this isn't my first rodeo, and the guys are in the lifestyle, too, after all. After searching his gaze for a minute, I shrug, nod, share a quick, chaste kiss on the lips with him and turn back to resume my seat on the rug.

Sinking deeply back into Littlespace with the others comes easily as I play, forgetting all about my previous need for the bathroom until my bladder insists that it's urgent. But, little and wanting to go along with Daddy's unasked request, I continue playing through it until the resulting dampness against my skin has me squirming with discomfort.

"Come on, sweetheart," Daddy's voice is warm in my ear. He's crouching at my side and gives me a huge smile when I turn my head to face him. "Let's get you changed, okay?"

He helps me to my feet and leads me down the hallway by the hand. In our bedroom, he's got a towel spread out on the bed, with a fresh diaper, wipes and cream all set out neatly beside it. The fact that he was prepared for this both surprises me and also reassures me that he's really okay with it. I mean, he must have been, to leap on the chance like he did.

Staying in Littlespace, I don't ask him his color. I know that if this does make him uncomfortable, he'll safe word if needed. So I lie back on the towel he's set out and suck my thumb, watching him with hooded eyes as he tugs down my play shorts and unclasps the onesie beneath. I arch off the mattress so he can push the fabric up my back, then drop back down when he requests it.

It's a practiced routine at this point, the only difference being that this time the diaper has been put to use. I can't describe why that makes it feel different, only that it seems more intimate somehow, but still just as *normal* as anything else we've done together.

I take a second to muse over the fact that it never felt this easy with Trent. The few times we did this had felt a bit awkward, and the reason why almost eludes me. Almost.

Trust.

Some part of me never quite trusted Trent completely. Like an innate warning system, my brain had always hovered on the edge of being big in situations like this, like I knew I couldn't just let go and give him everything. It wasn't that he was a bad person, but he'd been my first Daddy and we'd had to work hard at our relationship. At communicating. At avoiding fights. At maintaining a routine. It felt formulaic with Trent, where with London it feels natural.

I really don't have to work at any of those things with London. And letting go with him is unbelievably easy. Because I trust him.

I love him and I trust him inherently.

He's rolled up the wet diaper with efficiency by the time I tune back into his actions and has wiped me clean. His large hands smooth the barrier cream over my skin almost reverently. Then he gets me to lift my hips so the clean diaper can be slid under my ass and he fastens the tabs with practiced ease, making sure it's all fitting and sitting correctly before getting me dressed again. I sit up, thumb still in my mouth, and watch as he tidies away the supplies and throws the old diaper into the trash can in the bathroom. I hear the faucet run as he washes his hands and then he returns, coming to sit beside me on the bed, the mattress dipping with the action.

"Thank you for trusting me with that," Daddy says softly, pulling me in for a sideways hug. "I probably shouldn't have put you on the spot with everyone here…"

I shake my head, pushing out of my Little head space to have the necessary conversation. "It's not like it's something new or strange to any of them. I mean, Charlie and Ash disappeared for the same reason earlier." As the words leave my lips, I make the connection. I smirk a little, cocking my head as I turn to observe him. "Is that why you suggested it?"

He nods, a bit pink in the cheeks. "You know I've wanted to tick it off our list for a while. And Charlie…" he sighs and looks at the ceiling. "He and I discussed it from a Daddy perspective, y'know? And he has this whole spiel about the vulnerability and trust involved and I…" London clears his throat. "Alright, full disclosure: I got a bit jealous that I hadn't experienced that, I guess." With a rueful shake of his head, he looks back at me and takes my hand. "Except, in the middle of it, I realized that I *have*. It's in *everything* we do together. We're vulnerable with each other all the time, and we're constantly proving how deeply we love and trust each other. This was just another way of sharing that, but it's not the only way. Not that it wasn't like he said it was."

Every time I think I couldn't love him more he says something like this. Something that is far more mature and soothing than a man of twenty-seven has any right to be. I forget that he's so much younger than me when he's so perfectly authoritative on one hand and so nurturing on the other.

I don't know what else to say to him other than: "I love you."

We share those three words a lot, but it never fails to send a thrill up my spine when he returns them. Brushing his lips over my knuckles, London looks me in the eye and does just that. "I love you too, Matt."

And, in this moment, life is perfect. In a few months, I'll be forty-six. A year ago, I could never have imagined feeling this way. I can't pretend to know what the future holds for us, but I have confidence that, whatever it is, we're going to face it all together. Me and my hot young Daddy.

Epilogue – London

Matt and I survived the six-month trial of my flexible work arrangements and are celebrating my final bi-weekly return by going out for dinner. If Matt had it his way, we'd get takeout and celebrate in bed, but I want to show my boy off in public. It feels like it's been too long since I've spoiled him.

Plus, I get off on seeing him dressed up a bit. He's always hot, but in dress pants and a button down, especially paired with a tailored jacket, he never fails to get my engine running. I like to think of these outfits the same way he describes my lingerie: like wrapping paper covering a beautiful gift, and I look forward to being able to peel the clothes off him later in the evening.

Even though he's not going out in Littlespace, I still took care of all the decisions tonight. That's my role as his Daddy, and I take a moment to consider just how much I still genuinely enjoy it. From selecting his outfit, to choosing the restaurant, to pre-perusing the menu online so I know which meal to order for him. The fact that he trusts me to make the right decisions for him even now kind of blows my mind.

"Ready to go?" I ask him once I've tied the laces of his dress shoes, grinning up from my kneeling position on the floor. He nods and smiles, handsome as ever, and we head out of the house (locking the door behind us) and to my car hand-in-hand.

We talk about Matt's work week on the drive across town, which then segues into a summary of my last trip across the country.

"Stan and I agree that they're pretty autonomous these days," I tell him as I park my trusty little Hyundai in the lot next to the cute French bistro I decided upon. I unbuckle my belt and twist in my seat to face him, beaming because I'm so happy to report this to him. "So it looks like I'll be able to get away with visiting the office in person once a month at worst. The rest of the time, I can manage them remotely. Teams meetings, emails, that kind of thing."

Matt's expression lights up like a Christmas tree. "Really?"

I bob my head with enthusiasm.

"That's awesome!" He leans across the center console, grunting in complaint when he's stopped by his own seatbelt. His hands scrabble to unbuckle himself and I chuckle at his distracted fumbling. Then he takes a deep breath, shoots me an unimpressed glower, finally presses the button down and launches himself towards me.

His lips are on mine before I can blink, and he takes control of the kiss. It's deep, and passionate, and I lament the lack of space in my tiny shitbox car when I can't pull him any closer against me.

"We're going to be late for our reservation," I complain lightly when we come up for air.

Matt snickers. "Does that mean we can get takeout and go home?"

I attempt to reach behind him to swat at his ass. "Be good, baby. I want to take my beautiful boy out and make everyone jealous."

Even now, after over nine months together, the compliments bring a flush of pink across the visible strips of skin above his beard. It's still adorable as fuck.

"Fine, Daddy," he moves back into his seat with a playful pout. "But you're buying me dinner *and* dessert."

"Oh, sweetheart," I take the bait, "you *are* my dessert."

* * *

Dinner goes smoothly, and I know that, for all of his complaining that he'd rather be at home, Matt enjoys the rare night out. He practically moans over every bite of the meal I selected for him, the decadence of the French cooking too delicious not to enjoy.

We play footsie beneath the table, teasing each other like we're on our first date instead of in a committed, long-term relationship. And I do order dessert, because he's been such a good boy and I'll do anything to keep that smile on his face.

But when we get home and I pull into the driveway, there's a stranger on our doorstep.

In the passenger seat, Matt tenses up, frowning as the man who had been leaning against the wall next to the front door pushes away and moves towards us.

"Trent," Matt inhales sharply, and now I'm feeling tense as well. What is he doing here? Who does he think he is that he can just turn up on his ex's doorstep unannounced?

As Trent steps into the light from the motion-sensor flood-lights we installed above the front door, I can see that he's tall like Matt, and roughly around the same age at a glance, but lean and clean shaven. He has light-colored hair, something like a sandy blonde, and a long, angular face. As he gets closer and I climb out of the car having told Matt to stay put for a moment, I note that he's handsome in an ageing Hollywood star kind of way.

He stops and frowns at me. "And you are?" He asks, and his voice is higher pitched than I'd anticipated. Maybe this attitude is in compensation of not exactly having gravitas in his voice, but from the little bits and pieces Matt has let slip in our time together, I think it's more a case of Trent just being an asshole in general. Or maybe I'm projecting.

Pasting on a genial smile, I extend my hand. "London," I introduce myself. When he gives me a slow look over, starting at my feet and trawling slowly up towards my face, refusing to shake my hand or introduce himself, I ignore the distaste in his expression and cheerfully tuck my hand back in my pocket. Leaning back against my car, I cock my head to the side. "How can I help you, Trent?"

With a roll of pale blue eyes, he gestures at the car with a dismissive wave. "I'll talk to Matteo, thank you." He clears his throat when I don't budge. "Privately."

"Yeah, that's not going to happen," I bounce on my heels, remaining chirpy and overly friendly. "It's been, what, close to three years since you sent him packing without so much as a second's thought about how he was going to manage? You think he even wants to talk to you?"

Trent grits his teeth and I get the feeling he's not used to being challenged.

Well, too bad, cupcake.

"Listen, son," he patronizes me, "I've been sitting here waiting for almost an hour—"

"Well, that wouldn't be an issue if you hadn't turned up without so much as a courtesy call."

Rolling his eyes, he leans around me and loudly demands that Matt get out of the car and talk to him. Before I can insist otherwise, the passenger door opens and Matt climbs out. He's stony-faced and nothing like the sweet, jovial man I've spent the evening wooing and spoiling.

"Why are you even here, Trent?" He asks, sounding both defeated and disinterested. He walks around the car and I don't waste any time wrapping my arm around him, tucking him into my side.

Possessive? Yeah. Do I care? Nope.

"Really, Matteo?" Trent scoffs. "A boy of your own?" His tone seems to imply that he finds that concept ridiculous. Then he says, "It doesn't matter. We should talk."

It feels like I've stepped into a scene from a poorly scripted soap-opera. The inevitable 'ex-lover realizing that they've made a terrible mistake' moment. But, as amusing as that might be on paper, I can't help the stab of uncertainty I feel.

I can't help but worry that there's a possibility that Matt might prefer to go back to the man he has so much history with, after all.

Interrupting my thoughts, Matt laughs. An honest-to-God laugh of amusement. "If you think this man is my boy, you're an idiot," he says, shaking his head. "London's my Daddy, Trent. And he's a damn sight better at it than you ever were."

As he defends me, it's like I can actively see him getting closure on those painful years of his life. I can't deny the relief that sweeps through me at that. I nuzzle his neck, kissing him on the spot just behind his jaw that I know makes him all hot and bothered. "I'm so proud of you, sweetheart."

Trent just looks puzzled. "What?"

Matt shrugs. "I don't know why you're here after nearly three years of radio silence, and, honestly, I don't care." He turns his head to smile at me. "I'm in love. I have an amazing Daddy who treats me right and loves the way I look."

"Especially in a onesie," I add, and to my delight he giggles.

"Especially in a onesie," he repeats in agreement.

"But…" Trent starts, then stops. Matt and I look back at him almost in a synchronized movement. The man standing in front of us seems to slump in resignation. "So, if I told you that I made a mistake—"

"I'd agree with you." Matt's response is firm, but he still manages to surprise me with his undercurrent of kindness. I shouldn't be surprised, though. Not when I know how inherently compassionate he is. "Trent, we weren't good for each other. You were right to end things. If you hadn't…" he trails off and shakes his head. "It's been a long time. And if you're not happy, I'm sorry to hear that. I am. You're not a bad person, y'know?"

My sweet, forgiving boy.

He forges on, and it strikes me that he's probably been thinking about what he'd say to this man —his first Daddy— if ever he got the chance. "You realizing that you were wrong doesn't mean I'm going to walk away from the life I've rebuilt, but I would appreciate the apology. You did me a favor by letting me go, even if it took me a long time to see that. I'm doing you a favor now by telling you the truth."

There's an awkward silence between us all until Trent lets

out a sad sigh and nods. He has the grace to appear genuinely apologetic when he looks back up from the ground. He meets Matt's gaze first, then mine. "I'm sorry for disturbing your night," he says, and it's a far cry from the bluster and pomp of his initial attitude. I still don't really have it in me to scrounge up even a lick of empathy for him, but Matt has that covered.

"It's going to get better, Trent. But whatever closure you're looking for here? You're not going to find it beyond knowing that I'm happy."

* * *

I pin Matt to the door the second we're inside and his former Daddy is gone. My lips are on his in an instant, my hands tugging off his jacket and yanking at the buttons of his shirt. I don't care if I tear the damn thing, I'll buy him a new one. I need him naked. *Now.*

He laughs when I pull away to continue fighting with the material, and the sound is lighter and more carefree than I've ever heard him. "Daddy...I'm too old to fuck against the front door."

I can't even bring myself to admonish him for the language. I wrench his shirt off, buttons pinging and clicking and clattering across the tiles at our feet, then drop to my knees to mouth at his cock through the thick, black material of his dress pants.

"You're *perfect*," I tell him, my brain scrambled with need and pride and the resurgence of all the joyful, flirtatious feelings from dinner. I rub my face into his growing hardness, lavishing him with more praise. "The best boy, partner, lover...hell, you're the best *person* I could ever imagine."

His hand threads through my hair, caressing the top of

my head and I look up to see him staring back at me with amusement and adoration in equal parts. "You know, if I knew that telling Trent where to shove it would earn me this sort of reaction, I would have called him and done it ages ago."

Now it's my turn to laugh, and I shake my head. "It's not just that...but that was hot as fuck, by the way." I don't care how silly I feel making this declaration in this position. I have the fleeting, slightly feverish thought that if I had a ring, I'd probably propose, but despite the endorphins I'm feeling, I know we're not ready for that yet. But one day we will be, I'm sure of it. "These last few months have proven that we can work through challenges together, and every moment away from you has been awful. Tonight felt like the start of something new again. Something exciting."

I allow him to pull me back to my feet and I cup his bearded jaw with my hands. "And then, whether you realize it or not, just now on the front lawn?" I jerk my chin in the vague direction of the driveway, "You chose me. You could have listened to him. You could have had the age-appropriate Daddy you have a decade of history with. But, instead, you *chose me*."

His eyes soften and glisten with tears. "London," his voice is croaky, but he's smiling at me. "I'll always choose you."

Then we're kissing again, with the same intensity as before but at a slower pace. My manic energy is building into raw need and we make out while attempting to fumble our way towards the bedroom, shedding shoes and clothes (and his underwear and my panties, which involved a lot of hopping and laughter from both of us) in our wake. Glancing behind us, it's like a miniature disaster zone, the trail of a small, if passionate, tornado.

When we finally tumble into bed, we're finally naked and I

waste no time coating my fingers in lube and stretching Matt out. But, for as badly as I need to be inside him, connected with him at the most intimate level, I don't want to rush this. Instead, I plan to make love to him.

I guide him onto his side and press in behind him, lifting his thigh up and back over my hip so I can slide inside him at just the right angle. He sighs out my name, his hand reaching back to pull my face in towards him for an awkward, sloppy, utterly perfect kiss.

I set a languorous pace, rocking my hips slowly, dragging my cock out and in while I murmur everything and anything I'm thinking and feeling into the shell of his ear.

"You like that?"

He moans.

"You like it when I fuck you slowly, sweetheart?"

A needy whimper.

"You feel...*oh*," I gasp, "so *fucking* good, baby."

I push in deeper, practically melding myself to his back, as though I'm trying to become one with him. He's panting, his cock hard in my grasp, and now I barely move, just teasing him with tiny, incremental shifts of my hips against the perfect globes of his ass. "That's it," I practically croon as he tips his head back onto my shoulder, matching my minuscule moments, drawing out our mutual pleasure, "you're my good boy." I groan as I slowly push forward again, his tight heat driving me closer to the edge. "My perfect boy."

"Oh, God..." Matt hisses as I tighten my hold on his leaking cock, twisting on every torturously slow upstroke.

Despite the languid nature of our love making, my heart is beating rapidly and I can feel my balls drawing up, can feel my body giving in to the exquisite pleasure of being wrapped in his tight heat. "I want you to come for me, Matt," I tell him, engaging my best authoritative tone, the one I know he loves. "I want to feel you spurt over my hand. I want to feel your pretty little hole clenching around my cock. I want—"

He smothers a shout, letting go and complying with my request. I groan out my own release, spilling inside him, thrusting and grinding as I ride out every last possible moment.

I pull out slowly, kissing whatever parts of his face and neck and shoulder I can reach, then gaze down to watch as my cum dribbles out with my final movements.

It's insanely hot to watch. As hot as it was that very first night we spent together. Maybe even hotter, because this time we have the intensity of our emotions behind it. We have our own history, despite it only being nine months instead of a decade.

"Stay here, sweetheart," I whisper into his ear when I catch his eyelids drooping. "I'll clean us up."

I extricate myself from the bed and, while he's still dopey and malleable, get him to move so I can pull the soiled comforter out from under him, and the blanket beneath it to cover him up with once he's clean. Then I duck into the bathroom and nab a washcloth, warming it with hot water and wringing it out lightly before returning to find Matt has fallen asleep.

I clean him up gently, not wanting to wake him, then give myself a cursory wipe before I climb back in bed behind him. I curl up at his back, the two of us still naked, mirroring our earlier position. Pulling the blanket over us, I press one last kiss to his bare shoulder and snuggle in for sleep.

Tomorrow, we will discuss tonight's events properly. I'll repeat how proud I am of him for standing up for himself and getting his well-earned closure in a healthy, mature way. I'll also reiterate how touched I am that he defended me. That he chose me. That he said he'll *always* choose me.

The night I met him, I never could have imagined that he'd turn my world around the way that he has. I'd never imagined that being a Daddy was on the cards for me, let alone to a man nineteen years my senior.

I couldn't have anticipated that going home with him would lead to anything beyond a night of fun. Perhaps even a week or two at best. I certainly wouldn't have thought it would introduce me to a supportive social network of like minded people, or that I would be comfortable enough to be myself, open about my most secret (at the time) kinks.

But here we are: a Daddy who loves lingerie and a big, buff boy, in love and ridiculously happy.

And I wouldn't change a thing.

The End

* * *

Thank you so much for reading *Matteo's Mettle*. I genuinely hope you liked it as much as I enjoyed writing it. London and Matt took me on a ride I wasn't exactly expecting, going off the plan as soon as my fingers hit the keys. I think their story is better for it, to be honest.

I'd love it if you could leave a review on Goodreads and/or your favorite online retailer. Reviews not only tell the algorithms that our books deserve attention, but honest feedback also encourages and inspires me to keep writing. Even a star rating helps, and I greatly appreciate you making time to do so.

Speaking of my writing: if you're still enjoying the antics of the *Littles & Lace* crew, keep turning the pages for a sneak peek of Book 3 titled *Ted's Temerity.*

And, if you'd like a free ebook copy of *Charlie's Contentment* (a 10,000 word zero-angst, high-fluff novella which functions as an extended epilogue for *Asher's Answer,* but can also be read as a super sweet stand-alone) subscribe to my newsletter via:

https://annasparrows.com/newsletter-subscription/

For updates, release dates, competitions and more, follow me on Facebook. The link is in the 'About The Author' page after the sneak peek.

Sneak Peek: Ted's Temerity

Chapter One – Ted

"...to have and to hold from this day forward until death do you part?"

The question is quite solemn, but the officiant delivering them is anything but. The short, curvaceous woman is wearing a bright pink dress and her hair, cut into a spiky pixie style, matches it. She's bubbly and bright and is grinning at my best friend, Charlie, waiting for the guy to answer.

Seeing as I'm Charlie's Best Man, I give him a little nudge. In front of us, our assembled friends chuckle while Charlie clears his throat and finally answers with the only possible words he could. "I do." From where I'm standing, I can see that the sides of his neck and the skin on his jawline and cheeks not covered by his trademark dark stubble are turning a little pink.

The officiant winks at him and teases, "Right answer!"

Everyone laughs at that. Then she turns to Charlie's fiancé and asks the whole spiel again. I can see Asher's entire face from my spot behind Charlie's turned form. The younger man is practically vibrating with joy as he stares across at the man he's marrying. His curly hair has been trimmed and artfully styled, and his hazel eyes are shining brightly under the hot summer sun.

Thank God this is a casual wedding. The grooms are dressed in matching white linen short sleeved shirts and beige khakis. Matt and I, standing for Ash and Charlie respectively, are wearing the same pants, but short sleeved shirts in a pale blue color. It's late afternoon and there's enough of a breeze that we're not sweltering, but I'll be glad when this ceremony's over and we can crack open some crisp, cold bottles of beer.

Ash gives the same answer, the officiant declares them husband and husband, they kiss and we all cheer.

"Congratulations to you both," I drag Charlie in for a hug first, then Asher right after him. "I'm so happy for you."

Charlie pats me on my shoulder blade, but Ash squeezes me tight. "Thanks, Uncle Ted." I resist the urge to ruffle his hair. I can see that effort has gone into styling it today, and probably a bit of product besides. "Next time'll be you, right?"

I snort. I've known Ash for almost as long as he's been with Charlie, which is coming up on three years now. And in that time, while I've gone on a few dates from guys I met at The Grove, the local BDSM club, I haven't found the sort of connection that Ash and Charlie share. Additionally, there's a lot about my past that not even Charlie's aware of which, after close to fifteen years of friendship, would be difficult and painful to explain now. Instead, I focus on the obvious.

"I'm almost fifty," I argue with a shake of my head.

It's a mild exaggeration. I still have a few years before I hit that milestone, but it's sneaking up fast.

At Asher's questioning glance, I sigh. "I think I'm getting too old to believe I'll find someone to settle down with now." I shrug, forcing a bright smile that I hope meets my eyes. "But this is your wedding day, kiddo. Let's not bring down the mood."

Until recently, I was also Ash's boss in addition to being his and Charlie's friend. But he graduated college, having deferred and then studied part time after he met Charlie, and is now working with his husband. Together they're building a community hub for people like us: people in the BDSM lifestyle, with additional focus to those who enjoy the age regression kink. I've been helping out with some of the legalities, but Asher's business degree has proven useful for them, as have Charlie's connections from his previous career as a cop.

I'm significantly older than both of these men, but our social circle is eclectic. That's to be expected, considering we all met through the BDSM lifestyle.

Case in point: Ash's best friend, Matt, wanders over with his Daddy's hand clutched in his. To look at them, you'd assume the roles were reversed. They're both tall, broad men, with Matt eclipsing London in height and muscle mass. Matt's arms are heavily tattooed, and his neatly trimmed beard is more salt and pepper now than the brown it once was. The shaggy hair on his head, also neatly styled back today, is turning the same. He's roughly my age, so that's hardly a surprise. But his Daddy, London, is in his late twenties with thick, black hair and the flawless skin of youth. Like Ash and Charlie, their Daddy-boy relationship has been going strong since they met.

And, alright, if Matt could still find love in his mid-forties, maybe I'll concede that hope is not lost for me after all. It just seems unlikely.

"Congrats, guys," London gives the grooms each a quick hug before drawing Matt back against his side, "that was a really nice ceremony."

"Yeah, it was," Matt agrees, snuggling against his Daddy's shoulder. His tone is wistful and dreamy. "The weather was perfect, too."

We'd all expressed our concerns that choosing to marry in the park without a backup plan for bad weather was asking for trouble, but Ash held firm. He's quite stubborn when he wants to be. As if reading my thoughts, he casts me a smug little grin. "Told you it would be."

I shake my head. "You got lucky."

Charlie chuckles at that and tugs his new husband flush against him. "I'd say *I* got lucky," he says, aiming for schmoopy and disgustingly sweet.

Thankfully, his younger brother, Josh, has also meandered over from his spot amongst the guests. "Nah," he teases, "that's what your wedding night is for, isn't it?" He waggles eyebrows that match Charlie's for emphasis.

Charlie sighs with exasperation when we all snicker like teenagers. He shoots his younger brother a glare. "Fuck off, Josh."

"You wound me," Josh places a hand over his chest, then lunges for Ash. "We're officially brothers now!"

"He gets this from Mom," Charlie tells us as an aside, as though we're not all aware of the fact.

"Speaking of," I jut my chin towards the woman in question. She's bustling across the manicured lawn like a woman on a mission, practically dragging her husband (an older version of Charlie and Josh) along beside her. Charlie's baby brother, Axel, follows at a more sedate pace. Unlike his older brothers, Axel's short and stocky, with his mother's rounded facial features and curled hair. He graduated high school a couple of years ago, but still looks like a teenager to me. Then there's Charlie's sister, Maisy, and her husband whose name I can't remember. Charlie's family are lovely, but they're high energy and I'm already looking for my escape.

"Ted," Chance, one of the other Daddies in our little group, calls me just as Charlie's mother reaches us. I could kiss him. "Can you come help with the...uh..."

"The cooler," another younger man, one I don't recognize, steps in smoothly.

I try not to swallow my tongue as I look him up and down. I try to gauge his age and guesstimate that he's likely in his early thirties. He's immaculately dressed in a tailored suit (*in this heat? Is he crazy?*), all long limbs and big, dark eyes. He's got the prettiest smile I've ever seen, and his skin is, as Ricky Martin sang about a fictional paramour, the color of mocha. His voice is like liquid velvet, soft and sensual, and I'm too busy listening to the melodic tone to actually focus on the words.

"Sorry," I shake my head as though to clear it, belittling myself for the moment of infatuation. This man is beautiful but, even if he is kink friendly, the likelihood of him being a Little or wanting a Daddy as old as I am is slim to none. Assuming he's even single. "The cooler?"

"Yes," he looks amused, stepping in closer to me. "Can you come help with the cooler? We need to load it into the back of Chance's truck and it's just a bit too heavy for me to help properly." He bats insanely long lashes at me and I nod my agreement readily. Right now, I'd happily follow this pretty little thing anywhere.

My nameless savior apologizes to the grooms and Charlie's family for stealing me away, then leads me towards the parking lot. Finally getting my shit together, I look around for Chance, who we appear to have left behind.

Ah, well, he'll catch up. Thanks for taking one for the team, Chance.

"He said you'd need rescuing from Charlie's family," my companion tells me, interpreting my confusion correctly. "Unfortunately, it seems Chance isn't so great at improv."

"No, he's not," I agree, then stick my hand out to properly introduce myself. "Thanks for the rescue. I'm Ted."

Full, plump lips twitch upwards before he takes my hand. "Zephyr."

That...well, that was not at all the sort of name I was expecting.

Zephyr laughs. It's a surprisingly deep sound, considering the pitch of his speaking voice. "Yeah," he says, "I get that reaction a lot."

"What?" I try to recover. "I didn't say anything."

"You didn't need to. You had that 'how the hell does this guy have such a white boy hippy name?' look on your face. Don't worry; *everyone* looks at me like that." He shrugs. "My parents *are* hippies, by the way. At least at heart. I mean, Dad's an accountant and Mom's a teacher, but they're still very, uh, *creative*. So..." he gestures loosely over his lithe body, charmingly self-deprecating, "Zephyr it is."

Shoving my hands in my pockets, I rock back on my heels. "For what it's worth, I think it's a pretty cool name."

'Pretty cool'? Am I stuck in the 90s now? Why not just say 'rad' and really prove how lame I am?

Oblivious to my internal cringing, Zephyr smiles again.

"Thank you."

Awkward silence begins to descend. I don't want that. "So," I start, fumbling for conversation. I'm not used to fumbling. I'm usually cool as a cucumber. Suave. Sophisticated. "How do you know Chance?"

I want to facepalm as soon as the probing question leaves my lips. I might as well have asked if they're fucking.

Well done, Theodore. Walk away now before you really put your foot in it.

Zephyr, thankfully, throws me a bone. "Actually, I met him and Asher at The Grove." His posture is deliberately relaxed, but I can see him eyeing me for my reaction.

I nod and smile. "Littles' Night? Those are Ash's favorite." And when Charlie can't make it, Spence, Chance or I usually step in as his caregiver. I cock my head, looking Zephyr up and down slowly. "I don't want to assume…"

"Oh, I'm very much a Little." Once again, he takes me out of my misery. He looks me up and down, much the same way I just did to him. It makes me feel better about the exchange, like we're on equal footing. "I'd guess Daddy, but after Chance introduced me to Matt, I also don't want to presume."

"Definitely a Daddy," I nod, trying not to let my excitement over the basic compatibility between us show. Before the silence can descend again, I ask, "Are you new to The Grove?" I haven't visited recently, but I'd definitely remember seeing him around.

"Yeah. New to town, actually. Only been here a few months, and Ash…well, you know Ash." He laughs, shaking his head. "He wouldn't hear of me not coming to the wedding when he worked out how very limited my social circle here is, so…" Zephyr extends his arms out wide, palms facing the clear, blue sky. "Here I am."

I know my expression has turned fond as I think about Ash. He's flourished from the skittish, traumatized kid he was when he first stumbled into Charlie's life. And, because he knows what it's like to be lonely and to start over somewhere new, it's not surprising that he tries to welcome every new face with open arms.

"Well, I'm glad you came today," I find myself telling Zephyr, once again wondering where all of my ability to flirt and charm disappeared to. "And not only because you rescued me from Charlie's family."

It's a clunky save, but it'll do.

"Oh, is that so?" Zephyr practically purrs, stepping in a little closer. His dark eyes practically dance with amusement. "Why else would you be glad that I, a complete stranger to you, am here, then?"

Good question.

Before I can fumble over an answer that doesn't sound creepy as fuck, Chance interrupts us, throwing his arm around my shoulder while he grins at Zephyr. Chance's enthusiasm is usually infectious, innocuous as he is with his dad bod and ginger beard, but today the interruption grates on my nerves.

"Mission accomplished," he declares, sounding proud of himself. "Now all we gotta do is try and sit at the far end of the table at the fancy-schmancy restaurant you booked for tonight, and we can avoid Mrs Walker trying to marry us all off."

Honestly, considering the casual attire of the Wedding Party, it's not like we're going anywhere that exclusive, but I don't bother arguing with my friend. Instead, I allow his comment to launch us into a debate about the merits of getting to the restaurant early vs late, and I'm thrilled beyond measure when Zephyr agrees to ride with us in Chance's truck when we finally get our shit together and leave the park.

About the Author

I've been writing* for as long as I can remember. I started with silly short stories as a kid, moved on to fanfiction in my teens, and began publishing original fiction in my thirties.

I have been an avid reader of MM romance my whole life. (Ask me about my beginnings with *Buffy* fanfic, haha.) I wrote a sweet and kinky MM romance novel in 2022 and the reader response changed my life. From there, I knew I had found my niche.

And thus Anna Sparrows was born.

*All of my writing is 100% my own. No part of it is generated by Artificial Intelligence (AI) software of any kind. Yes, that means that it's sometimes flawed, but I'm okay with that.

You can connect with me on:

🌐 https://annasparrows.com

📘 https://www.facebook.com/AnnaSparrowsAuthor

📎 https://www.instagram.com/annasparrows

Subscribe to my newsletter:

✉ https://annasparrows.com/newsletter-subscription

Also by Anna Sparrows

I write ridiculously sweet & steamy MM romance with guaranteed HEAs…and sometimes with a side of kink.

Littles & Lace Series
The Littles & Lace series is an MM Age Play series, following a group of like-minded friends in the BDSM community. You'll find mild ABDL, light Pet Play, Femme Play and more here.

Book 1: Asher's Answer

Book 2: Matteo's Mettle

Book 3: Ted's Temerity

Book 4: Spencer's Satisfaction

Book 5: Chance's Choice

Book 6: Josh's Jackpot

Dads & Adages Series
Visit Australia's sunny Gold Coast where an assortment of single dads find love and even learn a few life lessons along the way.

Book 1: Where There's A Will

Book 2: You Don't Know Jack

Book 3: A Match Made In Evan (release TBA)

Shifters Sanctuary Series
In a world where alphas are thought to be extinct, a number of 'human' men are about to have their worlds rocked.

Book 1: His Alpha Unlocked

Book 2: His Prodigal Alpha

www.ingramcontent.com/pod-product-compliance
Lightning Source LLC
Chambersburg PA
CBHW070609120726
47909CB00007B/2506